The Misadventures of Slim O. Wittz, Soft-Boiled Detective

A collection of **8** Short Stories

By
Rosemary and Larry Mild

Magic Island Literary Works • Honolulu, Hawaii • 2014

Individual short stories appearing in *The Misadventures of Slim
O. Wittz, Soft-Boiled Detective* originally appeared in the following issues of *Mysterical-E:*

Slim Chance . . . . Fall 2009
Statistically Slim . . . . Winter 2009/2010
Slim and Nun . . . . .Spring 2010
Slim at Heart . . . . Summer 2010
Slim Pickings . . . . Spring 2011
Slim Down . . . . Winter 2011/2012
Slim Jim . . . . Spring/Summer 2012
Slim and Trim . . . . Fall/Winter 2012/2013
(Reprinted by permission)

Interior book design by **Larry Mild**.
Cover Art by **Jackie Mild Lau**
Cover design by **Marilyn Drea**, Mac-In-Town, Annapolis, MD.

Library of Congress Cataloging-in-Publication Data
Mild, Rosemary P. ; Mild, Larry M.
The Misadventures of Slim O. Wittz, Soft-Boiled Detective
Mild, Rosemary P. ; Mild, Larry M.

ISBN 978-0-9838597-9-6

First Edition 2014
10 9 8 7 6 5 4 3 2 1

Dedication

For our beloved grandchildren—
Alena, Craig, Ben, Leah, and Emily

For our wonderful children—
Jackie and Myrna

For our marriage—soul mates, partners, lovers

Acknowledgments

We could fill an entire volume with the names of all the family members, dear friends, and acquaintances who are loyal fans of our books, essays, and short stories. And you, our readers, are all precious to us and give us the ultimate push to continue our writing.

We want to thank **Joe DeMarco,** Editor of *Mysterical-E,* for his enthusiasm in publishing the eight Slim O. Wittz short stories in *Mysterical-E,* on-line magazine.

We especially thank **Sisters in Crime/Hawaii Chapter** for their continuing encouragement and expertise.

Our grateful thanks also to **Judith A. O'Neill,** our former mystery course teacher and good friend.

And many thanks to **Marilyn Drea** for her valuable publishing assistance.

Disclaimer

The Misadventures of Slim O. Wittz, Soft-Boiled Detective is a work of fiction. The plot and the events therein are of the authors' imagination and invention. All characters therein are fictitious and any resemblance to persons living or dead is purely coincidental.

Table of Contents
The
Misadventures of Slim O. Wittz, Soft-Boiled Detective

Story One
Slim Chance

MY NAME IS SLIM O. WITTZ. I'm a shamus, a private eye, and I'm at Voluptuous's desk signing reports. Yeah, Voluptuous! That's my secretary's name. Vo says she was born with that moniker. I'll give her the benefit of the doubt, though you could also add Volcanic, Voracious, Vociferous and Voluminous. They all fit.

If you ain't out dodging bullets, you're dealing with killer paperwork. My pen bumps into something under the document I'm trying to sign. I know what it is even before I look. Vo has been clipping her nails again. How many times do I gotta tell that dame it ain't dignified here in the office. I finish signing the top report and weigh the sheet in my hand, wondering whether Vo's extra coats of Wite-Out warrant more postage. When I interviewed her, she said she could type. I took her at her word. But after I hired her, she warned me that if I faulted her typing, she'd sue me for sexual harassment. Logic and Vo don't always make good partners. The brain waves in her lovely platinum blonde head don't always reach their destinations. On the other hand, the screwy logic could be her *modus operandi*. Maybe that's the only way she can get an employer to keep her on. But never mind. I stomach her steno screw-ups on account of her hourglass measurements and gorgeous gams.

The godfather clock next door chimes nine times, and I can see from my office through the frosted glass to the corridor that the second floor is deserted. I tell clients: Turn right when you step out of the elevator. It's the eighth door on your right. I have to remind people to count correctly. You see, my ex-brother-in-law, Elmer, is a sign painter. He counted wrong and painted my name on the wrong glass door. You'd think he'd have had a clue when he had to scrape the word "MEN" off first. I gotta wonder how many clients I piddled down the drain that way.

Apparently, I didn't learn my lesson with Elmer. I gave him fifty bucks to rent a bloodhound for a manhunt I'd been hired for. Did he go to the reputable kennel I sent him to? No way, Jose. A friend lent him a broken-down hound and Elmer pocketed the fifty. The useless pooch had a sinus condition the size of Delaware. The only thing that hound could smell was himself.

The office phone rings only once before I pick up: "Slim O. Wittz, Private Investigations. Neat, Complete and Discreet! Oh, hi, Mom."

Mom ain't really my mother. Actually, she belongs to my ex-wife, Fawn. I got custody of Mom after the divorce. Mom likes me much better than Fawn. To tell the truth, if she was twenty years younger, I'd have married her instead. But socializing ain't on her mind tonight. As I listen, an ulcer sprouts in my gut.

"Wait, Mom, I don't want anything more to do with Fawn. Mom . . . No!"

It's useless to argue with a desperate woman. Fawn dumped her boyfriend. He was always beating up on her and messing with her head. Her body's wallpapered with welts and bruises. Even though she booted him out and changed the locks on her doors, the guy won't leave her alone. She's afraid to go out and can't sleep at night. Mom wants me to lean on this creep and get him to move on. On the phone she coaches me. Like I really need lessons.

"I'm counting on you, Slim. Let him know he can't get

away with that kind of behavior. Maybe even rough him up a bit. Get him to cease and desist, if you know what I mean. It's the least you can do for someone who once loved you."

Although I doubt any lingering love on Fawn's part, I shrug my shoulders, say I'll look into it and hang up.

Intimidation calls for more than chewing the ape out, so I pull open the top drawer of my desk and reach for my piece. It's a vintage World War II .45 caliber automatic that I picked up last Saturday at a yard sale—tagged "As is. Ammo not included." I'm not sure it'll fire, even after a thorough cleaning. I scratch a memo to Vo to put bullets on my shopping list, along with a bottle of aspirin. I throw on my tweed sport coat, tuck the piece in the back of my belt, and head out.

My '93 Buick Regal sits at the back of the lot where I left it. The car is a dull gray, with numerous silver duct-tape patches to hide the rust. I'd prefer a newer set of wheels, but the kind of work I do says I gotta stay inconspicuous. Okay, truth is, I'd rather drive one of them snazzy Eyetalian jobs, but business could be a little better.

I'm hoping the pit bull what owns the lot has left for the night. But as I reach for my door handle, two rows of busted teeth grin out at me from the driver's seat: "You owe me two months' parking and you ain't leaving with this tin beast 'til you pay up."

"Have a heart. I ain't slept in my own bed for a week now."

He shakes his eight-ball head. It's then that I notice he's parked another jalopy in front of mine, so I can't get the Buick out anyway. I figure on pulling the smug S.O.B. out of my front seat and working him over. The runt reads my mind. He's got a fist wrapped around a tire iron, tapping it gently against his other palm like a cop with an itchy night stick. Under the circumstances, I decide to reconnoiter another strategy. I hot-foot it back to the office, where I wrestle another night with my Castro Convertible couch. At some point the half-nelsons, headlocks, and mattress-pins put me down for the count.

Next thing I know, Vo is leaning over me, shaking the living daylights out of me. A powerful aroma of cologne, lipstick and hairspray makes me almost pass out for good. I pop one eye open and find myself staring at the Appalachians. I didn't know the Cumberland Gap was that deep.

"Hey, sleepyhead. Ya wanna talk with your ex? She's on the phone."

"Not really." But I shuffle to the phone in my socks anyway. "Yeah!" I grouch into the mouthpiece, taking my miserable night out on her. "Yeah, so it's morning. What of it? . . . Don't thank me—I ain't done nothing yet. . . . Fawn, I said I would. What's the matter—my word ain't no good anymore? Where do I find this schlemiel? . . . What's that address again?" I write it down. "I'll let you know. . . . Now don't go trying all that sweet stuff on me. . . . Yeah, yeah, I'll call you." I hang up.

Mom told Fawn I'd take care of her stalking ex-boyfriend, so she's making sure I won't change my mind. That's the trouble with dames. They think you forget them as soon as they're out of sight. They're wrong. I think about dames all the time.

But how come I feel so achy? I finally figure it out. I fell asleep with the gun still tucked in my belt. It left a bad impression on me, and now I'll be sore all day with this .45 caliber pain in my backside. I tell Vo to add a shoulder holster to the shopping list— just as soon as we get a few more receivables.

A shave and fresh shirt help me back to feeling human again. Mom promised me a meal later, seeing as how I'm doing her this favor.

I shove the piece into my jacket pocket and head for the elevator. On the way down, I glance at the address Fawn gave me. It's walking distance, about five blocks away. Pinsky's Haberdashery. Mom told me the ex-boyfriend has two jobs. The haberdashery is his day job. I didn't ask what Rocco's other job was. Yeah, Rocco, at least that's what Mom said his name was. Probably a harmless nickname.

I push open the glass door into Pinsky's and waltz up to

the only salesman in sight: a short, stocky buck I make out to be in his late thirties. Good looking and a sharp dresser, too. Kind of resembles me. Hmm . . . I can see why she'd fall for this dude.

I'm thinking this intimidation job is gonna be a cinch. I can't figure how Fawn could be afraid of this guy. "You Rocco Vinnelli?" I ask in the gruffest voice I can muster.

"Naw, I'm Max Pinsky, the owner. That's him coming in now."

It takes seconds for this image to register. The locomotive entering the store comes at me in chugs. I decide Arnie Swartzenbagel's got nothing on Mister Vinnelli. Except for the hair. Rocco's Saint Bernard mane would make Beethoven jealous.

"Hey, Rocco," Max greets him. "This gentleman's been asking for you."

"Hi. What can I do you for? Hey, just a joke, pal. How can I help you?"

I clear my throat and throttle back the gruff tone. "A friend told me you'd fix me up with a new sport jacket. Said you'd treat me right."

Rocco grins broadly and motions for me to follow him to a rack of sport coats. I shed my threadbare jacket and hang it on a hook while he opens a spiffy tan job with brass buttons for my arms. As I slip into it, the key question keeps mulling around in my mind: How do you intimidate anyone six-four and 250-plus pounds?

The jacket's tailored for Godzilla, but Rocco insists that it's right for me. I feel his paws gripping extra material behind my back.

"As close to a perfect fit as you can get for your kind of figure," he says smugly. "Room to grow, too. You don't want to take all the sport out of sport coat, do you?"

Not daring to argue with a hulk towering half a foot over me, I ask whether he has something in blue, something that would take a few years off me. At forty-one I feel like I've crossed over a bridge that's collapsed behind me. But I don't tell him that. He nods, and I try on a few more jackets—that is, I actually try to try them on, but I can't even get both shoulders in at the same time.

"A bit skimpy," Rocco admits, "but that's the style these days, especially with the younger bunch. You did say you wanted younger." He figures he's lost the sale by now, and his glued-on smile begins to fade.

Just so he won't think I've come in here for another reason, I ask if he expects any new merchandise. He tells me maybe next Wednesday, then reaches for my own jacket to help me into it. But as he picks it up, he feels the added weight. His pork-sausage fingers fumble through the pockets until he retrieves my .45 automatic.

He levels it at me. "Who the hell are you? No one goes this kind of shopping with a gun in their pocket. What are you up to?"

Max, quietly arranging ties on a display table, beats a retreat into the back room.

Rocco is one angry goon. He spins me around and slams me, face forward, over the counter so he can get at my wallet. My P.I. badge and I.D. card take him to another level of furious. "Who sent you? Was it Angel? Does he have a contract out on me?"

If this is a test, I don't have any answers. I speculate about Rocco's second job. He endures about half a minute of my silence, then shoves me toward the front door.

"Hey, Max," he shouts in the direction of the back room. "Cover for me. Gotta go out for a few minutes." And me he asks, "Where's your car, Scumbag?"

He ain't at all happy when I explain that I didn't drive over. He prods me toward a red Coupe de Ville parked at the curb. It has that dazzling look of a brand-new, freshly heisted car.

"Get in," he snarls. "No, Stupid, on the driver's side."

Rocco reaches under the driver's seat and comes up with the keys. He hands them to me. I start the engine, slip into gear and roll the Caddy away from the curb. It's the first time I've ever driven one of these pimpmobiles. He points the piece at me now as he gives directions on how to get out of town. I comply. What else can I do? I keep glancing at the gun, which looks a helluva lot more menacing now than it did in my desk drawer. I don't mind being pistol whipped with my own gun so much as I dread the dental bills afterward—worse even than novocaine. You see, I let my dental insurance lapse. Not a good idea for a person in my profession.

After driving for thirty-five minutes, he has me turn onto a deserted road, steeply graded and full of switchbacks. Not a house in sight. I follow it uphill for another three or four minutes, and then he tells me to pull over and stop the car. I choose my place just beyond the crest of the hill, with a panoramic view of the town in the distance, and pull way over onto the grass. I turn off the engine.

"Okay, Bozo, get out. You didn't come into the store for no sport jacket. What's this all about?"

"It's about Fawn, Rocco. She may be my ex, but I still don't tolerate anybody beating her up. You hurt her. Gave her two black eyes. Slapped her around in public. And that was just the first week. She called it quits with you, but you won't take No for an answer."

"Get this straight, Bozo. Someone's tellin' you stories. But just to keep the record straight, I never lay a hand on her, not that kinda hand. That babe's too independent to stick around a bad dude. You ought to know. Fawn left you, didn't she? And as far as I'm concerned, she's still my woman."

Rocco puts the gun to my head. He's taken the safety off, but I know for sure there are no bullets in the clip, so I hustle out of the driver's seat and slam the door. The thug tries to get out on his side, but I've pulled so close to the guardrail that he can't get the passenger door open. He swears big time—nothing I ain't heard, mind you, but he does it with such pizzazz. From his passenger seat he again aims the piece at me, but awkwardly now. Pulling the trigger several times, he gets click, click and click for his efforts. He flings the gun through the open window. Lucky for me, his pea-size brain doesn't think of it as an excellent blunt instrument.

Now he wants to come after me, but because of his bulk, he's got trouble maneuvering across the console to the driver's side. It'll be minutes before the gorilla can perform that trick.

I don't stick around to find out how long. I dash around to the Caddy's trunk and heave my sizable backside into it to coax the car down the hill. I don't know if it's the adrenaline pulsing through me or the Cream of Steroids I ate for breakfast, but the beautiful red machine begins to roll. You see, I had a bit of a plan when I got out. I deliberately didn't set the parking brake and intentionally threw the shift into neutral.

Rocco is bellowing, roaring now. He's made it across the console and is struggling to reach the driver's side door. I throw my whole weight against the trunk and shove once more, straining, sore back and all. The car continues to roll.

The grade falls more steeply here. Now the car takes on a life of its own. With the steering wheel still angled slightly toward the guardrail, the car scrapes against it, creating sparks and a terrible rasping noise. In spite of the friction, the vehicle picks up speed. Suddenly, it slams into a guardrail post and careens back onto the open road. I watch the coupe build momentum to ten, maybe fifteen miles an hour toward the next downhill switchback. Blam! Crunch! It cuts clean through the fence and disappears from view.

Impact. Then silence. It all kinda spooks me. I'm not proud of what I've done. Not that I feel for that creep, mind you. It's just that I normally don't do the killing thing.

As I slowly drag my out-of-shape carcass back up the hill, I spy my .45 lying in the road where Rocco had tossed it. I pick the piece up, dust it off, and check it over. It feels lighter—the ammo clip is missing. I search all over the road and shoulder, but the clip's gone like yesterday's supper. I slip what's left of the piece into my pocket and continue walking. Now I'm thinking about the dinner Mom promised to make for me. Roast beef with Yorkshire pudding, I hope. It's her specialty. Before long, I'm sweating like a perp collared in the act, and the idea of a cold shower nudges any thoughts of food aside. When I reach the main road, a semi stops for me and I hitch a ride back to town.

Eight hours later, scrubbed like Mr. Clean, I ring Mom's doorbell. She lets me in, but slowly. No hello—just an annoyed look on her puss like I'm a Hoover salesman. Voices from the dining room reach my ears. I find Fawn already seated at the table. And sitting across from her is the individual I least expect to see in Mom's house—or anywhere: Rocco. He rears up out of his chair. Hell, it ain't my night to get pulverized, so I pivot and skedaddle to the front door as quickly as my stocky legs allow.

"Wait!" Mom cries. "Come back! I can explain everything."

I gotta be nuts 'cause I shuffle back into the dining room, shaking worse than Fawn's personal vibrator. Mom points to a chair across from my ex, whose baby blues and pouting lips still get to me. I lower myself into the chair and listen to Mom. Turns out, Rocco isn't the guy I was supposed to intimidate. He's Fawn's new boyfriend! Rocco's boss, Max, is the abuser, only Mom got the names all twisted, and I went after the wrong galoot. Rocco's face is decorated with a scratch from one ear to his mouth. But the rest of him looks to be in perfect health for a gorilla in captivity. He does me the honor of an explanation.

Would you believe, Rocco says he just wanted to put the squeeze on me some and teach me a lesson, so he took me out in the country to make me walk back. He was madder than a bee without a hive when I made my break for it. Sure, he fired the piece to stop me, but he knew all along the gun wasn't loaded—he'd put the clip in his pants pocket.

"What about the wheels?" I ask.

Chomping down on a carrot stick, Rocco grumbles, "The Caddy kept goin' through the fence at the switchback. On the other side of the fence it slowed down and mugged a tree.

Fawn pipes up in her usual sorrowful squeak: "And you got hurt, too."

"It ain't so bad, toots," Rocco tosses off. "Just a scratch." He wags his finger at me. "Hell, it ain't my car. It's Max's. He knows you're the guy responsible for totaling it."

Oh-oh! I figure Max will be siccing his lawyers on me by morning.

Rocco smirks, enjoying the doomed look on my face. He says, "No sweat. Max got the message and won't be bothering Fawn anymore. He says he ain't suing and he don't want to mess with Slim O. Wittz neither."

So Max thinks I play too rough. Well, I'm not about to change his mind. I ask Rocco: "Ain't your boss pissed at you? You still got a job?"

"Yeah, but I'm more pissed at Max for what he done to Fawn. Besides, I got something else lined up." Rocco offers his paw across the table. "How 'bout you and me calling it even?"

We shake on it, and I assure him that Fawn is his turf from now on. If she wants to be, of course. He grins and pushes the empty ammo clip across the table at me. Somewhere between navy bean soup and Mom's main attraction, I learn that Rocco's second job is arranging centerpieces for a florist.

I help myself to a slab of roast beef.

Statistically Slim

THE GLASS ON MY FRONT door reads "Slim O. Wittz, Private Investigator." How I became a shamus ain't all that exciting. Let's just say I got a smell for it. As for the moniker Slim, I ain't no Sidney Greenstreet—just a shade pudgy, but I'm working on it. I'm trying to eat all the right things, too. There's a catch, though. How the heck can I take time from a stakeout to go food shopping? What if the cops catch me spooning away on some diet yogurt, or the bad guys find rice cake crumbs all over my lap? I'd never live it down. Those guys are like elephants—they don't ever forget.

Voluptuous, that's my secretary's name. The leggy blonde with the turquoise eyes and firehouse lipstick smile answers to the name of Vo. That babe has got real smarts too—she even goes to night school. She's got the big desk over there by the window—something to do with her plants. Besides, she spends more time in the office than I do. Vo supposedly works for me, but she don't do groceries, coffee, or windows. That's because she's one of them liberated-type dames. So I gotta find the time to shop for myself. Maybe it's just as well. I know what I like. Besides, that broad would be substituting stuff she thinks I need.

The case I'm working on don't have a paying client, unless

you count me. I'm the client here because there's some kind of conspiracy going on and yours truly is the victim. Know what I think? You can put the yellow crime scene tape around the whole damned supermart down the street. Yeah, something's weird at the Gyant-Lyin store. Stuff that I need is always disappearing from the shelves. The rest, the stuff nobody in their right mind would buy, stays on the shelf forever, collecting dust. And that ain't the worst of it. Whenever I enter one of them aisles between the goodies, I get this weird feeling that someone's put the tail on me. It's like someone's giving me the once-over all the time, keeping track of what I buy. Then the next time I come in to get the same item, it's flown the coop. Swoosh—like magic, my favorite thing is gone. No reason given, just swoosh.

It began even before I went on my diet. I remember the day the bristles started to fall out of my hairbrush. I like using a man's brush instead of a comb—it's gentler on my scalp. Anyhow, I need a new brush, only now there ain't any on the shelf where they always were before. The clerk tells me they don't make 'em anymore. I outsmarted them that time by getting a shoe brush. If I hear another crack about shining up my bald spot, I'll pop you one. I got this receding hairline all right, but mind you, I ain't no Yul Brynner neither. And try to find a polo shirt with pockets now that cigarettes are out of vogue. Where am I supposed to keep my glasses?

Frozen desserts—Lite, Fat-Free, Lo-Carb, and on and on: they're my biggest gripe. Every time I find a flavor I like, Abracadabra! It goes missing like my grandpa's teeth. Then there's the White Fluff toilet tissue issue. The manufacturer swiped every last roll, but left a note, "Try our Cutsie brand instead." I never did see the sneaky crook, the Benedict Arnold, not face to face, anyway.

I was squeezing tomatoes over in produce and mumbling about my losses, and this gorgeous tomata with the luscious melons overhears me. This dame with hair the color of ripe red rhubarb claims it happens to her, too. Whew! I thought this thing was a personal vendetta. Don't know how widespread this caper is. It may be spreading to other stores, like measles. Then, again, she might just be making conversation.

Today I come prepared. I bring this dish towel with me, so when I covertly slip a box of Applenut Triangles off the shelf and into my grocery cart, no one can see me do it. I'm usually pretty good when it comes to sneaky capers. Sometimes, even I don't know what I'm doing. Suddenly, some tall geezer in a trench coat ambles down the aisle, hesitates near my cart, and attempts to look over my shoulder. I block his view, so he can't see bubkes. He moves on and disappears around the corner. Swiftly, I tuck the Applenuts undercover. Just then, some skirt sashays down the aisle behind me carrying a bundled blanket over her shoulder. She seems to be just strolling, but directly opposite my cart, she stops, shifts the bundle to her opposite shoulder, and flips up the blanket. What do ya know? It's a baby wearing a hidden diaper-camera! Yech! Something smells in Denmark. Is her mom taking a picture of me and my cart? Good grief, look who's getting paranoid now. She and her baby spook slip out of sight behind the Pampers pyramid.

There and then I make this big decision to follow her. I leave the cart behind and hurry to the end of the aisle. The skirt and sure-shot tot are gone. I check a few more aisles—vanished, just like the bowl cleaner stuff. By now I'm more frustrated than Tom Dewey in '48. I head back to my cart only to see a short guy with a clipboard stop at my cart, give it the once-over, and then tiptoe to the next break in the aisles.

"Hey!" I yell. "Hey you! Stop!"

The guy keeps moving, then he too disappears. I run after him. At the break I look left—nothing. I look right—nothing. And then I look down at my feet. This short guy with the clipboard is sitting on the floor between the sauerkraut and the relish, all curled up and shivering like a beach bunny at the North Pole.

"Don't hit me. Please don't hit me." He cowers with his hands over his face.

"Why would I hit you? What were you doing in my cart?"

"I didn't take anything. I swear it." He lowers his hands, revealing a bald head and a small round face flushed nearly the shade of the ketchup on the shelf behind him. Nervously, he straightens the black bow tie on his short-sleeved white shirt.

"Then why were you there?"

"I'm taking a survey?" His voice trails up at the end.

"That sounds more like a question. Ain't you sure?"

"Honest, it's the truth. Why would I lie?"

"How should I know?" I ask. "Maybe if I take you outside and rough you up a bit, you'll come clean with me."

"No, no, don't do that! I'll talk."

"Go ahead then, talk. My ears are listening."

He clears his throat. "I had to find out what products you selected. It's what I'm paid to do."

"Why pick on me?" I ask.

"I can't help it if you live in a test area and you're one of our statistically perfect samples," he whines.

"How come if I'm so perfect, you keep pulling my favorite stuff off the shelves?"

"You're not like any of our other samples, sir."

"Do you work for the store?"

"No, sir."

"Well, who do you work for then?" My simmering temper edges toward a rolling boil.

"A private consumer testing agency."

"They got a name?"

"Consumer Habits, Inc., sir. They're one of the biggest."

"And nosiest. Let me see your clipboard."

He clutches it close to his chest: "Oh, no, sir, that's top secret. If I let you look at it, your inadvertent bias will ruin a whole universe of statistically correct data. I can't let you do that. My reputation and the company's will be trashed. Our credibility will fall below that of the former President of the United States."

"You can't, eh?" I stare at him with my steeliest eyes and begin to rub my hands together as though I have finally reached the fun part.

He slowly pushes the clipboard toward me. "Well, if you promise not to tell anyone that I showed it to you."

I make no such promise. Instead, I snatch the board from his shaking hands and take a gander at it. "Where'd you get my name and telephone number?"

"I found your check underneath the cash drawer in register number six."

My blood pressure pushes up the bulb. "I expect my business transactions to be between the store and me. My name, address, telephone number, and selections aren't up for grabs. What ever happened to privacy?"

"You don't have any, sir," he blurts out. "There's this law that says your privacy belongs to anyone who asks for it—unless you deny it specifically in writing and provide additional personal data, including your Social Security number and your mother's maiden name."

I shake my head and lift the cover sheet on the clipboard, expecting to find some other poor schlemiel's sheet directly beneath mine. I don't find any other completed sheets. "Why is this only about me and my choices? Why aren't there any others in this survey?"

"The undisputed results from the last survey indicated that you are the perfect statistical sample."

"You already mentioned that."

"I know. The results showed that you clearly represent the group that chose those products least likely to succeed. So I was selected to observe your shopping habits exclusively. Anything you choose is subsequently pulled from the shelves. The company finds it cheaper that way. Surveys cost big bucks, and I came up with this way to save money. I got a raise, too."

"And how do you think I feel about this—all my favorite things taken away from me? Mr. Negative—that's who you think I am." This little pipsqueak has gotten under my skin and he's going to pay for insulting both my good taste and intelligence: "Get up!"

I command. I grab him by both shoulders, wrench him to his feet, spin him around, and push him toward the back of the store.

"Where are you taking me?" he squeals.

"You'll see. By the way, what's your name?"

"Why do you want to know that? Are you going to get me in trouble with my boss?"

"I wanna know why the brand of what I'm taking off the shelf is your business. So are you gonna tell me?" I squeeze his shoulders harder with my fingers—so hard my nails dig in.

"Ow! It's Frank, Frank Whimpert! Please, you're hurting me."

We reach the rear of the store and a large white door.

"Go ahead," I growl, "open it. Both of my hands are busy."

The wuss looks up at the sign on the door and nearly melts into his socks. The sign reads "Trash Compactor."

Just inside the door I prop the little guy up and drag him to a chair. I pick up an empty soda can from the recycle bin and toss it into the compactor. The machine senses it and makes this grating, booming, and crunching noise as the metal is sucked into its gut. Wimpert's frightened eyes pop wide at the noise.

"Know what?" I snarl. "I want out of this damn survey thing. You go find some other patsy for your fun and games."

"I g-g-get your drift, sir. M-m-maybe I can help you."

"Oh, yeah? This I gotta hear."

"M-m-my boss has a warehouse. She buys up job lots of the stuff taken off the shelves and retails them as rare commodities at exorbitant prices."

"That can't be legal," I protest. "Who would buy such merchandise?" I throw another can in the mechanical mouth to maintain Whimpert's level of interest. Scrrrunch! Ka-boom! Poof! Swoosh! The can is sucked into oblivion, and the impact on my hostage is spellbinding.

Whimpert looks away from the bellowing compactor, then back at me. "My boss has a whole list of statistically perfect losers— you should excuse the expression—like yourself. Now she's doing them a favor, offering to sell them the missing products, and the losers are very willing to pay. My boss lives quite high, so she must be successful. She's definitely defrauding the product manufacturers. The selling part is more than a stretch, and her pricing scheme sure is pushing the envelope."

"Where's this warehouse of hers?" I have another used soda can ready, but instead of throwing it in, I merely flip it around in my hand. I have his complete attention now.

"It's near the tracks. I hear trains when she phones me from there."

I gotta know more about this broad, so I ask him, "What's she look like?"

He tells me she's a looker—stretched-out, leggy, and a sharp dresser. He adds that she's got a load of shiny black hair and wears it loose. I tear a blank form off his clipboard and tell him to write all the particulars about his boss and her office address on the back. When he finishes, I turn a grateful Frank-the-wimp loose.

That night I call the boss at her home. Her name is Merle Irons. I give the dame my name and explain I'm one of her statistical samples. I don't want to get Whimpert in trouble, so I tell Miss Irons I got her name and number from one of the other sample suckers who want to remain anonymous.

"Can I see some of your merchandise, check out all your goodies?" I ask.

"Down, boy, can't do that, hon." Her words float out of the phone like a mellow cello. "What did you have in mind?"

I give her some examples of the precious items I've been missing from the shelves—a man's hairbrush, polo shirts with pockets, White Fluff tissue, fat-free cherry-chocolate yogurt, et cetera. I'm too embarrassed to tell her about the Geritol, so I omit it from my list. Miss Irons murmurs sympathetically, but says I can't come to the warehouse. She'll call me when she gets the stuff I mentioned—should be sometime tonight. We agree on pricing, and she hangs up.

I need to get Bessie, my '93 Buick, out of hock. The thirteen-year-old buggy is ready for its Bat Mitzvah. So at the office I borrow some money from Vo, who gets a ten percent pay hike if I don't return the funds by the end of the month. The collateral's got me by the gonads, but there's no arguing with that broad.

I hightail it over to the company address that I weaseled out of Whimpert. I park across the street a few doors down and wait in the car for Miss Irons to emerge from her habitat. It's a two-story brick office complex with head-in parking for five cars. The lettering on several windows of the second floor tells me I got the right address. I'm here because I need the business and I think I can sell my investigative services to some or all of the product manufacturers she's defrauding. I don't think their management will appreciate anyone nixing perfectly good items just to sell them in an underground market.

Since I don't know how long I'll have to wait for this dame, I start munching on a stale slab of mushroom-and-spinach quiche. Wouldn't you know it, as soon as my mouth is full, I see a bozo in uniform making like a toy soldier. He's coming over to my car. I'm parked in front of this luxury apartment building, and the door-man may have some objections to my being there. I dump the crumbling quiche in my lap and await his greeting.

"Move that multicolored pile of junk out of here, buster. Can't you see this is a respectable neighborhood?"

I ignore the diss to my trusty wheels, reach under the dash-board for an old garage door opener, and shove it against my right ear. My lips silently recite "Mary Had a Little Lamb" for his ben-efit.

"Sorry, officer, hadta make this emergency phone call, so I pulled over to the curb to make it safe." I salute him respectfully with my left hand and continue the ovine-speak with the garage opener.

The doorman wants to say something more challenging, but finds his brain in a traffic jam with his mouth. So he shakes his head, puffs up his chest, and marches back to his precious station. Like a Catskills comedian says: "Doormen are part door."

All the while I keep an eye on the Consumer Habits office on the second floor across the street. There's a light on, and a window is open. I finish off the finger-food mess on my lap and brush the crusty remainder onto the floor. Suddenly, this vision of loveliness comes to the front window, reaches up, and slides it shut. She scans the street below and then cuts off my peep show by pulling the blinds. A minute later the light goes out, and quicker than you can say Dashiell Hammett, the door to the street opens and Merle Irons herself pours into view, only partially covered by her plunging peasant blouse and mini-skirt.

My eyes track the young goddess with the Pantene hair. Approaching a yellow Firebird, she slides her chorus-girl legs in and roars away. Apparently, the excitement is too much for my Bessie. She coughs, then floods. After two more tries and a half-minute wait to the tune of a few choice words, her engine catches. I rumble off down the street and ease in behind the Firebird at the first traffic light. When the light changes, I tail at a professional distance. I don't want this dame to get suspicious.

Merle leads me across town at a leisurely pace, and soon I see the train tracks. We cross over at Hickory Street and take the first right. She stops in front of a huge cement and corrugated steel warehouse. I extinguish my lights and park at the corner. Merle sheds the Firebird, climbs the concrete steps, and unlocks a metal security door. As soon as she disappears into the building, I'm out of my car and tripping up those same steps. Through a grated window, I see a distant light come on, maybe in another room—at least, I hope so. Luckily, the only other lock is a deadbolt, and since the dame didn't relock either one after herself, I slip in behind her.

The first room is darker than a coal miner's lunchroom and filled with cartons of every shape and size—the missing products, I presume. The light in the distance is shining from a makeshift office propped up on a ten-foot platform with a flight of grillwork steps going up to it. I hear a rotary phone being dialed and then the goddess gabbing on it, but not what she's saying. I slip in behind a row of palettes containing giant cartons and creep behind them to the left edge of the building. I then snake my hefty torso forward along the not-so-new and non-improved stuff until I'm in the space just under the office.

I can hear pretty well now, and what I hear disturbs me. The beauteous Miss Irons seems to be dealing in smuggled Asian antiques and using the nixed product business as a front. On the phone she's spelling out all the specifics. She even repeats the Swiss bank account number as she jots it down on paper. I thank my lucky stars I take my Ginkoba regularly, so I easily memorize all the incriminating stuff. She hangs up and dials again. This time the subject is about a ship, the *Ito Maru*, due to dock on Friday. I can hear only one side of the discussion, so all I can figure out is they're working out some pickup arrangements.

The area is dimly lit by an EXIT sign with a broken lens, and I see my shadow projected onto a carton of Oxydol soap powder sitting several feet in front of the steps. I quickly move away from the light to crouch behind an open carton of Ipana toothpaste, but in my hurry I stomp on some broken glass. Immediately, the talking stops, and she ends the call. I hear her move out onto the staircase landing. Her magnified shadow tells me she's toting a small-caliber piece. I can see her just above me through the open grating. By now, I'm wishing I'd brought my .45, but statistically, this isn't the kind of case that calls for firepower.

"Who's out there?" Merle booms, in percussion this time. No more mellow cello. She sweeps her Beretta back and forth, covering the entire warehouse floor. "I know you're out there. I can hear you. I've got a gun, so you'd better show yourself."

I open the Ipana carton and slip a tube of toothpaste out of its box. Waving the tube in front of the broken EXIT sign comes off like I'm pointing a gun, and the effect ain't lost on Merle. She squeezes off three quick shots at the moving shadows and starts down the steps in her stiletto heels. Silently, I creep forward. Through the open steps, I reach for her nylon-covered leg and latch onto her ankle like a mongrel chomping on a Porterhouse bone. She screams as her body topples forward. I let go, and she bumps and tumbles down the remaining stairs. She drops the piece. It slides across the open floor, lodging out of reach beneath a loaded pallet.

I have to admire this view of Miss Irons sprawled out cold on the floor in front of me. Aside from the fully exposed gams and bikini undies, I check out the rest of this dame. I ain't no Dr. Kildare, mind you, but I don't find any fresh blood or serious head injuries. Merle starts to come around now, moving all of her limbs, so I figure there's no broken bones either. Awake, her first move is to cover up her sudden exposure—just when things were getting interesting.

Hoisting Merle to her feet, I prod her back up the stairs to the office. Lucky for me, I find a spindle of heavy duty packing cord on the desk. I truss her up like a heifer—my special delivery package for the cops—and pick up the phone to call them.

"Hey, handsome, put down the phone and let's talk. Don't you want to know what's in it for you?"

She's playing her sweet tones again and I'm her audience. "What're you offering, toots?" I smile back at her.

She forms a smooch on her lips, like I haven't swallowed enough of her bait yet.

"Me! All of me, honey, and there's always a slice of the pie, pretty boy."

Now I ain't the most moral and honest citizen around. Sure, I like operating between the sheets just as much as the next hombre. And I might try to use a postage stamp more than once or take a good poke at somebody, but this smuggling business is out of my league. I got some scruples, in spite of what you might think of me.

So don't go getting your patooties all in an uproar—I call the cops. The suits with badges get here about twenty minutes later, and I spill the whole shebang. It turns out to be the big break in a case they've been milking for months. For the most part, they're grateful. But one bust-your-beeswax suit hauls me in on a breaking-and-entering charge. I never get along with this long-toothed galoot. So I make my one allowed call to Vo at her home. I tell her to come down with a lawyer and bail me out.

Near midnight, Vo, in a classy pants outfit, shows up alone at the precinct just before I'm tossed in the holding cell.

"Where's my lawyer?" I demand.

She fluffs her platinum blonde curls. "Not to worry," she whispers in my ear. "I'm a second-year law student."

My secretary, would you believe, begins to question my accuser. "Was there a sign on the door indicating that it's a place of business?"

"I suppose so," the galoot replies. "But it was after hours."

"Were those hours posted anywhere in sight?"

"Not that I noted," he snaps.

"Were you aware that the door was left unlocked?"

"How the hell would I know that?"

"You got in, didn't you?" she counters.

"I suppose so. What are you—some kind of lawyer or something?"

"Yeah, something," she answers "Don't you think your evidence is kind of thin? Where's the breaking-in part?"

The galoot reluctantly unlocks my cuffs and shoves me toward the door. I want to give him a piece of my mind, but Vo signals for me to keep what's left of it out of trouble. I realize now why I pay her a decent salary. In addition to her delicious looks, she's got a bundle of smarts and she's a mouthpiece to boot—well, almost one, anyway.

As we walk out, I slide my arm around her curvaceous waist. She throws me this stink-eye look and wiggles free. Just my luck—she's taken off the shelf, too.

#

Story Three

Slim at Heart

HEY, YOU CAN CALL ME SLIM, Slim O. Wittz, and I'm one of them old-fashion private eyes. Yeah, I'm a dinosaur, a shamusaurus, a leftover from the nineteen thirties and forties, only I can't claim to be so tough. I've got me a rented office over on Second Street upstairs from Leo's greasy spoon and one of them fancy bakeries called La Patisserie. It's sort of like going ten rounds with temptation every time I enter or leave my building.

It's evening and I'm sitting on a counter stool downstairs in Leo's, devouring a plate of dripping ribs and crunchy French fries, when the story on the above-the-counter TV strikes my eyeballs. It seems some big-time, low-life corporate CEO is about to be jailed for bilking his company employees out of their retirement funds. It's in the millions. Now this Wilkie Ponze character has already been tried, convicted, and sentenced. But his darling trophy wife, the former Missy Cushymam, says the poor dear can't possibly go to the pokey because he's too sick—he's got a weak heart. The appeals judge says he's taking that under consideration.

The news bite shows the two of them coming out of the courthouse. Missy's all eingaputzed with designer duds and dia-

23

mond jewelry. Grinning, too. Wilkie's in a dark three-grand suit and a solid tie. The joker looks like class even if he doesn't behave like class. The camera zooms in. He grimaces a sour puss full of perfect teeth like a hissing cat and pushes his thick-lensed, horn-rimmed glasses up from the end of his nose real snooty-like for the cameraman. I'd believe in a used-car shill before I'd trust a face like that. Also, his bald pate shines like a mirror in the sun, but I guess that part ain't his fault. Then the video switches to the VIP cell they got reserved for this crud upstate, and I can't believe what I'm seeing: two single beds pushed together, an easy chair, a TV set, fancy plumbing, and—get this—an outside window and carpeting.

Somehow, I can't feel sorry for a crook that cheats his own people, so I rip off a hunk of rye bread, swish it around in the remaining gravy puddle, and plop it into my mouth. I do this like I'm striking a blow for justice, even though it ain't me personally getting screwed. The sopping bread tastes so good going down that I turn my attention to the sporting news. The word ain't so good there neither—my Washington Redskins are eight and seven and now out of the NFL playoffs. In disgust, I push my plate of nude bones away and pick up the check, $19.53. Highway robbery! I put down the exact change and ten percent more. I always leave ten percent: it tells them they're good, but there's lots of room for improvement. The waitress gives me her usual evil eye and bids me goodnight.

I don't even make it to the door of that illustrious establishment when I feel the first symptoms. It's like some invisible goon is squashing my chest. I can't breathe. I'm hurting big time. As a shamus, I've been shot at, stabbed, beaten-up, bear-hugged, and mauled—it never felt anything like this. I'm gripping my chest like it's gonna explode. I nearly pass out leaning against the counter for support, so the waitress calls me a cab. I bet she's hoping it ain't their coffee. She helps me into the back seat, and the driver asks, "Where to?"

I tell him, "Hospital emergency room and step on it!" He looks at me strangely.

Repeating my request doesn't seem to help. I finally make out this guy doesn't speak American. I'm thinking he's new in this country and has only had a couple days behind the wheel. I figure the only words he can say are Where to? and Pay up. And the only ones he understands are Go straight, Right, Left, Next block, and Stop here. I use this quick-study vocabulary to get us there. He drops me at the ER entrance, and I pay what shows on the meter, withholding my usual ten percent. After all, I did the navigating.

I stagger out of the cab holding onto my chest and push through the big glass doors. The crowd inside the reception area makes me feel like I've walked into a U-3 rock concert. I worm my way through the hordes up to the reception desk and tell the chick in blue, "I'm having these chest pains." The next thing I know some male nurse swoops in from behind and hauls me off to one of them curtained cubbies about the size of two phone booths. The bruiser then heists me onto an examining table. Now I'm looking up at blaring lights and a bunch of white-coated, fuzzy mugs staring down at me, fussing and fiddling around with IV tubes, stethoscopes, EKGs, clipboards, and blood pressure cuffs. I feel like a plate of chicken livers with everyone drooling over me.

At least three different voices are screaming questions at me: "Where's the pain? What's your name and address? On a scale of one to ten how bad is it? What's your Social Security number? Have you had this kind of pain before? Who's your next of kin? What meds are you on?"

Everything's hazy. I answer what I can—feebly. All this tumult over me and I can't even enjoy it. So what do I do? I zonk out. I don't remember another thing until late the next morning when I wake up to this beeping sound. I'm in a barf-colored room with tan Venetian blinds. Beeps are coming from a six-foot Frankenstein on wheels. When the cobwebs clear, I see it's a monitor screen and I'm not happy with the program. Wavy bright lines are traveling from left to right, and I can't change the channel. I cough, and the lines go wild. I hold my breath, and the bottom line gets smaller and changes shape. Wow, reality TV. What power. I try to move and I suddenly realize I'm wired for sound—at least eight wires are attached to my chest. The bed's so soft and squishy, I got mucho trouble rolling on my side. I'm a prisoner in my bed.

The nurse comes in to check on me, but won't tell me a thing except "You've had a heart attack, and the doctor will be in later to explain more." Now there's a mouthful to stew on for the next three hours. She's got a built-in frown and starched boobs, so I can't get any more out of her. I make a face at the ogre, and she stares me down over the top of her granny glasses. What ever happened to TLC?

That afternoon the good ole Doctor Welby type finally sticks his head in the room and reads the riot act to me: "Got to change your life. Get off your butt and exercise more." I have this cornball image of me jogging in place while I'm on stakeout. "And no more fatty foods and desserts either." That makes me wonder if chewing on a crisp carrot stick can be done quietly when you're doing a little eavesdropping. The doc, a trim fortyish guy with gray beard and rimless glasses, turns out to be a pretty square apple and tries to explain what happened the night before.

It seems that after I conked out, they took me up to the operating room and tried to install a spring-like "stent" gadget in my right coronary artery. He says he entered the blocked artery on my right thigh next to the family jewels and continued up to my ticker. I peek under the sheets, and sure as taxes, it's all black and blue down there. But he ran into trouble and couldn't get past a tricky twist where the artery zagged and turned into what he called a shepherd's crook. And here I always thought shepherds were good guys. They're in all the Bible stories, ain't they?

"Jeez, so how long have I got, Doc?" I ask with my jaw sitting on my chest.

"Not to worry," he tells me. "Your heart attack was in the early stage. It's a small artery. Medications will do the job of unblocking it. No surgery needed. Get plenty of rest and exercise."

Rest and exercise? Sounds like the sawbones is speaking with forked tongue. Rest sounds pretty good to me, so I try to buck the hospital's keep-you-awake program. You know—vital signs every three hours, medication every four hours, and sleeping pills at two ayem. Since sleep is impossible with the beeping monitor, I try to look for hidden melodies in the chorus of beeps coming from it and other rooms on my floor. As you might guess, bed-panning is not my favorite activity either. I gotta say the chow ain't too bad—only they ain't never heard of salt and pepper. Otherwise, the only relief comes when Voluptuous, my secretary, brings me the morning paper, or my ex-wife, Fawn, phones in to gloat, "I told you so years ago."

The routine lasts two days, and then I'm transferred out of Intensive Care to room 506 on another floor. There I get a personal monitor transmitter clipped onto my hospital gown and orders to march the hall in that most dignified apparel with rear exposure. As soon as Vo—that's what I call Voluptuous—brings me the morning paper, we start meandering the halls together. Down the hall from my room, there's a cop sitting on a chair by the door to 511. Now this gets my curiosity up, so I ask the candy-striper patrolling the halls with her newspaper cart. She's just left the local fish wrapper in room 511.

"Oh, that's Mr. Ponze, Wilkie Ponze." she responds giggling. "Don't you read the papers?" She picks up the front page and points to a picture of Ponze turning himself in to the DA.

The Ponze name sounds familiar, so I rack what's left of my brain and come up with that scum CEO from the TV the other night. Inside room 511 there's someone sitting up in bed reading the spread-open paper, but I can't see what he looks like. My nosiness gets the cop's attention, so I give him a silly grin. But before he can say anything, Vo and me continue on and make a complete hallway loop.

On the second pass, I get a better look at the patient. By now this cop's shooting me the poison eye. This time the patient's newspaper is folded back. The cop gives me the bum's rush by way of clearing his throat. The patient hears him and turns to face us. I notice three things. First, the guy does look pretty much like the husband in the TV close-up, except there's some prominent gold dental work showing that I don't remember seeing before. Second, the scum's reading and he ain't wearing any glasses. Strange, guys with thick lenses usually can't wear contacts. Third, his obviously shaven head is showing dark stubble and gray scarring all over. I remember the close-up of the guy on TV as being permanently bald—what they call a polished pate even.

I lean toward Vo and whisper, "Hey, something's rotten in Denver."

"Denmark!" she says loudly. "Something's rotten in Denmark. It's Shakespeare."

"I know, I know, but not so loud. You want him to hear us?"

"Who, Shakespeare? He's been dead for years."

"No. That guy Ponze in the room there." I'm motioning my head toward the open door.

When we get back to my room, I send Vo on a few errands. Half-an-hour later a nurse, a real looker this time, sashays in to tell me I'll be able to go home the next day just as soon as the doc checks me out. I make a lame pass at the babe, but she chooses to forego the opportunity. I'm heartbroken, but I figure my hospital-ization won't cover it.

Sure enough, on Tuesday afternoon I walk out of the joint and into Vo's car. She drops me off out front at the office and goes shopping for her mother. Ignoring the café and bakery, I step into the corridor between them and trudge up the stairs to the second floor. About halfway up, I'm thinking I shoulda taken the eleva-tor—I'm pooped when I finally get to the office, so I lie down on the Castro Convertible to recover.

I spend the rest of that day and all of the next holed up in the office with Vo bringing my meals and the local fish wrappers. It's more convenient for us here 'cause she lives just down the street, and I'm not supposed to be driving yet. Besides, business is slow, and there's two or three surveillance reports I gotta get out or the rent don't get paid.

On Friday morning between gulps of decaf and spoonfuls of soggy Bran Krisps, I see that this Ponze scum has made the papers again—big time. He dropped dead two nights ago in his hospital room from heart failure. The funeral is slated for this afternoon at three. While I'm reading, I'm thinking the bum got what he deserved. But then I get to the end paragraph where his uptown lawyer says the family's gonna appeal and likely get the conviction overturned. Their appeal is based on the wife and kid shouldn't have to suffer just because the dad was a criminal. Now this gets my chest in an uproar and my ticker racing, and that ain't good for a guy in my delicate condition. I can feel the tension building under my ribs, so I reach into my pocket and shake one of them nitro dynamite pills from the teeny brown bottle and slip it under my tongue. Whew! That's playing it close to the chest.

If this legal shyster gets his way, the Ponze family won't hafta pay bubkes to the employees he cheated out of their retirements. At the sentencing, the judge promised the poor schnooks at least fifteen cents on the dollar from the remaining family assets. Now they'll get zilch, nada, nothing. If there's no conviction, there ain't no crime and no need for either payback or damages.

For a few days I didn't think about the hospital and what I saw in room 511, but now it's all coming back. Naw, it couldn't be. Nobody's that slick—hiring someone to die for you? Sheesh! I don't know where all my sudden energy comes from, but I think I gotta help the workers Ponze cheated. I call Vo and tell her to get her buns over here and meet me downstairs, lickety-split. While I'm waiting, I tear out the phone book page listing travel agents and run off a couple copies of the newspaper photo of Mr. and Mrs. Wilkie Ponze. I'm thinking they're about to go on the lam, and the family car would be out of the question. I'm guessing somewhere overseas—maybe a country without extradition, a place with secret banking accounts.

Vo arrives, and I give her an address. Before you know it she's winging me crosstown in her red and white Mini Cooper. She asks if I'm comfy, and I tell her I like riding around folded in half.

I take one look at the Yellow Pages' enormous list of travel agencies and decide I'm wasting my time. Mr. and Mrs. P. wouldn't go to a reputable agency, and paying without plastic would attract too much scrutiny. I have to assume they already have their phony passports and credit cards, possibly for months now.

There are three sources of phony plastic and passports in town, but Kenny the Kite tops them all. I redirect Vo to the Kite's address, and when we get there, I tell her to wait outside. Kenny's a short, stocky hood with glasses—and a real artist. He did time for forgery in the seventies, but went straight for a bunch of years running a photocopy and stationery shop. When computers and the competition from the large office supply chains put the squeeze on him, he started doing odd jobs again to stay profitable. I guess it would take a steamroller to keep Kenny straight. Yeah, the cops know all about him, but keeping him in business is one way of keeping tabs on the unsavory in this town—not that Kenny tells all, mind you. The more profitable stuff falls through the cracks now and then. The Ponze job was going to be one of them things until I walked into his shop.

Kenny owes me from way back—an alibi thing where I saved his crooked tail. Today I'm calling in my marker. I wait while he tends to another customer, except that he keeps giving me the stink eye, like I'm making him nervous. When the customer leaves, I show him the newspaper photo, and he knows for sure that I got him dead-to-rights. Kenny always keeps records of his illegal transactions, so when he's really put on the spot, he can claim his so-called honest intentions to report them to the police. It's worked so far.

With a minimum of arm twisting, Kenny shows me the file on the Ponzes, only it's marked Angello and Marie Massimo. I look at the passport photos. Sure enough, it's them—only Wilkie is in a faded Hawaiian shirt with rimless dark glasses and wearing a jet-black toupee. And Missy Ponze's hair is no longer blonde and curly—now it's brown, cut close, and feathered. Artist that he is, Kenny admits that he aged the passport covers and added a few visa stamps for authentication. I have this itch that Angello Massimo might be someone real, so I decide to scratch my itch and see what falls out.

I get lucky—the phone book has an Angello Massimo over on Taragon Street. I thank Kenny and remind him of his civic duty to report the Ponzes at least by the next day, and he catches my meaning right away. "Yeah, tomorrow, boss," he says as I walk out of the store.

Vo is doing her homework when I get back to the car—papers spread all over the front seat. You see, she goes to law school nights and works in my office three days a week. I shove the papers into a pile to make room for my butt, and give her the Taragon Street address. She slips the pile into her briefcase and pulls away from the curb.

We arrive at the garden apartments on Taragon Street, and I knock on the door, but no one answers. I knock louder several times with the same result. Then the door across the hall opens and a voice behind a cloud of cigar smoke says, "Yeah, whadya want?"

"We're looking for Mr. and Mrs. Massimo."

"Angello's moved out and dare ain't no missus, so far's I know," says the smoking voice. "I'm the resident manager." His cigar pops up and down with each word.

"Is there a forwarding address?"

"Naw, las Satady he jus paid up da tree mons back rent and skeedaddled outta here. Dint even pack a grip."

"He didn't take anything with him?" asks Vo.

"Nuttin'. Da place was funished, Wasn't nuttin' persnal left eida. Musta tossed it all."

"Mind if I have a look at his flat?" I ask. The cigar rolls around in his mouth, winding up on one side, and he gives me this What? Do-you-think-I'm-crazy? look like I'm gonna trash the joint. I slip out one of the two remaining sawbucks in my wallet and hold it out to him. He hesitates and scrunches up his face. Hmm, not enough, I think. As soon as I free up the second ten spot, the gonif grabs them both. Then he unlocks the door.

Angello has left the flat in pretty tidy order. All the drawers, shelves, and closets are empty. We're about to give up on the joint when Vo decides to pick up the telephone handset with her hanky and press the redial button with one of her long painted nails. She holds the handset away from her ear so we both can listen.

After several rings, a female voice answers, "Hello!"

I take the phone from Vo and respond, "Marie, Marie Massimo?"

"Yeah, that's my name. What do you want? I'm a busy woman."

"My name is Wittz and I'm a private investigator."

"So?"

"I'm calling from your husband's apartment."

"Ex! My ex-husband. Angello and I are divorced."

"I'm afraid your ex might be mixed up in a scam that I'm investigating."

"Damn! I knew that big certified check he sent us was too good to be true. He's always doing something shady. That's why I divorced the dumb lug. It isn't any way to bring up kids."

"I wouldn't go spending the check just yet," I tell her. "The police are going to be very interested in it."

Marie is less than anxious to cooperate, but when I outline the scam to her—especially the part about Angello dying for someone else, she comes around. "I knew Angello was sick when he phoned Saturday morning. He sounded awful, but he didn't want to talk about it. He wanted to make sure I got the cashier's check."

Before we hang up she gives me the name of the certifying bank and the address of the so-called Mr. and Mrs. Massimo.

The next stop for me and Vo is Police Precinct Four, where my poker buddy Lt. Barbara Harker runs a bunko squad team. I figure we got the goods on this Ponze creep, but we need Barb's help in making the actual arrest. Barb meets Vo and me at the reception desk, and we follow her back to her office, a dingy ten-foot square with pea-soup walls and no windows. She leaves the door open for ventilation and turns off the chugging window AC so we can hear. Barb sure ain't a looker, but she's got a tall wiry body to go along with her shrewd mind and keen eyes. Inside, she's got a heart that's soft and gushy, a real pal.

Barb takes notes while I clue her in on what's going on. I can almost hear the gears crunching in her straw-blonde head as I come to the part where I suspect Angello Massimo's corpse might be lying in Wilkie Ponze's casket during this afternoon's funeral. When I'm finished with my tale, Barb makes a few phone calls—among them, one to the appeals judge for court orders. The first is to allow the Ponze funeral to proceed, but to hold the actual burial until the coroner's office has a look-see. The second is for the airlines to release manifest information on a Mr. and Mrs. Massimo. On this one the judge takes a little more convincing, but Barb makes a good case for both orders, so Hizzoner comes through. Barb makes one more call to the coroner's office on the first floor, and they agree to send one of their people along to the funeral parlor.

While we wait for the airlines to respond, I tell Barb about my heart attack, and she gives me a big bear hug and the same lecture I got from my doctor—like it's some kind of broken record. Hey, she's a good friend and means well. The phone rings and she announces that Mr. and Mrs. Massimo are booked on Caribbean Tropics Flight 43 leaving 8:33 tomorrow evening. Since my good watch, a Timex, is visiting Sam's Pawn Shop, I pick up Vo's wrist and turn her hand so I can see the time—two minutes after twelve noon. Assistant Coroner Dr. Ralph Morse is waiting for us at the bottom of the stairs. The four of us squeeze into Vo's Mini and head for the courthouse to pick up the court orders.

It's close to 2:30 by the time we arrive at the funeral parlor. Just as we park, a black stretch limo pulls up to the canopied front entrance, and Missy Cushymam Ponze, in her finest basic black sackcloth, slides to her feet, shuts the limo door, and glides up the steps to the door. There's a black veil covering her new unblonde hairdo. I tell my companions it's weird that a liveried chauffeur doesn't get out and service his passenger. The limo moves to one end of the lot and occupies three parking spaces. The chauffeur lowers the seat back and pulls his cap down over his face, obviously planning to nap. I casually follow on foot until I get opposite the driver's window. Barb and Dr. Morse go inside to serve the court orders to the funeral director. Vo prefers to wait in her Mini.

"Hey, good buddy, you got a light for my cigarette?" I ask the chauffeur. He springs upright, allowing the cap to slide from his face and revealing his polished bald head. The fake mustache doesn't fool me either. I now have no doubt who this bum is, but I got all I can do to restrain myself from dragging him out of the driver's seat and giving him a knuckle sandwich. He nervously pushes in the dashboard lighter and when it pops out, he holds the glowing tip toward me. I lean over with the cigarette in my mouth and light up. I mumble "Thanks," and walk away quickly so he doesn't get his suspicions up. I meander over to the Mini and slip in on the passenger side next to Vo while we wait for the funeral to end. I squash the cigarette out quickly, as I gave the nasty habit up ten years ago.

Forty minutes later the few mourners start to trickle out of the parlor. Then Missy, complete with lacy handkerchief dabbing at her eyes, comes down the steps all slow and respectful-like and heads for the limo at the back of the lot—no door-to-door service for her. A few feet behind Missy, I see Barb tagging along with a grin on her face, and she gives me the high sign. I get out of the Mini and approach from the opposite side.

When Missy reaches the limo, Barb grabs her purse and tells her to put both hands on the hood. Ponze reaches for the key in the ignition and tries to start the vehicle. I think he's about to run over his wife, so I yank open the driver's door, haul his butt out onto the tarmac, and put one foot on the creep's chest. Barb is busy cuffing Missy. When she's done, I grab the chauffeur by the collar and drag him to his feet so she can cuff him as well.

"What's going on here?" he cries. "I haven't done anything wrong."

"Wilkie Ponze, you're a convicted felon," Barb responds.

"Technically, an escaped felon also. And now your wife is afoul of the law for aiding and abetting your escape."

"How could you know all that? The coffin was closed."

"True," she answers, "but when Dr. Morse from the coroner's office opened the coffin, he found the body had a mouthful of gold and silver dental work. And if it weren't for Slim O. Wittz here, you might have gotten away with your scam. Your press photos gave you away."

"Yeah!" I pipe in. "Your teeth bit off more than they could chew."

#

Story Four

Slim and Nun

YOU CAN FIND ME IN THE TELEPHONE BOOK under
private investigators—Wittz, Slim O.—right after Wilton, Hubert
B. They don't have a proper section for shamuses or gumshoes,
not even a See Private Investigators listing. But that's what I do for
a living, and I'm good at it. Voluptuous has the notion that she's
more than just my secretary. I let her think so because it's cheaper
than giving her a raise. Yeah, Voluptuous. That's her name and she's
got the soft curves to prove it. Her turquoise feline eyes, sculptured
nose, and full baby lips don't hurt her looks none either. Besides,
her being a law student is like having a get-out-of-jail-free card on
the payroll. It's Vo's bright idea to advertise in the book.

The word's out that I'm a throwback to the gumshoes of
the nineteen thirties and forties. You know, the likes of Sam Shade,
Flip Marlow, and Mike Slammer—the hard-boiled private eyes
with the hidden honest streaks and deep soft spots for the hard-
bodied damsels in distress. In reality, I prefer mine over easy—both
my eggs and my women. Mostly, I investigate errant spouses: the
unfaithful, the gamblers, the embezzlers, the runaways, the otherwise missing, and the meshuga kind.

I answer the jangling phone. "Slim O. Wittz Investigations...Yeah, pound and a half... lean... a pound of Swiss... half-

dozen rolls… a round rye. Sure, right away." I hang up.

My telephone number is one digit off from a delicatessen's and I'm constantly annoyed by all the wrong numbers. Callers have a helluva lot of chutzpah. They get pretty nasty when I can't tell 'em the right number. Don't they even hear me say "Investigations"? So now I'm accepting orders and being very polite about it. Sometimes I say I'll throw in an extra side of slaw or a slab of halvah. When they get hungry enough, I figure they'll learn to use the phone book. Meanwhile, I've put on twelve pounds just from listening to all the food orders.

As a Jewish private eye, what would you think my chances are of getting involved with a shiksa, let alone some holy Catholic woman? I'd say slim to none. Yet three weeks ago, after finishing four straight days of stakeouts, I'm resting my head between my folded arms on the desk when I hear this persistent banging on the office door.

"It's open," I yell, picking up my head. "You don't have to break it down!"

A gentle woman's voice answers, "There are no lights in here."

"Switch is by the door," I tell her.

As my eyes get used to the light, she asks, "Slim? Slim O. Wittz?"

"Yeah, that's me. How can I help you?" In my clearer vision she begins to look sort of familiar, but I can't quite place her.

"Lily McElvee from high school. Don't you recognize me?"

"I'll be damned," I reply. "Silly McElvee. I never expected to find you in my office."

"I've always hated that nickname. If I remember correctly, you're the one who tagged me with it."

"Guilty as charged," I say, jumping up from my desk chair. "Why don't you get rid of those wet things? There's some hooks behind the door." I'm ready to give her a huge hello hug. But as she flips back the hood of her coat, I get a shock. She's wearing a nun's headdress—black, draping to her shoulders. Her brunette bangs form a fringe below the headband. Then she sheds her rain jacket and I get another shock. No nun's habit. Just a slender figure in a trendy denim skirt and white blouse.

"I'm Sister Maria Leona now." Behind rimless glasses she levels her blue eyes at me and smiles, friendly-like. "You look a little confused."

"You got that right, Silly, I mean Sister. Jeez, uh, this nun thing. No white wings? No long robe?"

She chuckles. "Sally Field I'm not. Besides, the Flying Nun was forty years ago. It depends on the Order we're in, but the traditional habit has pretty much gone by the wayside for many of us."

Maybe, but I ain't going for the hugging thing and offer her a chair in front of my desk. She surprises me with a matter-of-fact squeeze anyway. Really confused now, I return to my swivel chair. "Well, is this a social visit or is there something I can help you with?"

"I'm afraid I'm in need of your professional services, Slim."

"I always thought you gals went upstairs for this kind of help."

"This particular problem is more earthy by nature. It has nothing to do with the Church. And, don't worry, this isn't a charity case. We can pay."

"I charge $550 per day plus expenses. For you, I'll waive the thousand dollar retainer fee."

"Thank you."

"You said *we*. If not the Church, who are *we*?"

"My sister Melba and me."

"A Sister's sister—sounds complicated. So what's it all about?"

"Twenty-six years ago I joined the Holy Order and I didn't see much of Melba for some years afterward. I can't say who was more at fault, but we lost touch anyway, and I felt bad about it. Through some friends I learned that she had become a bookkeeper in Las Vegas and had found herself a satisfying life."

"It sounds more like the end of the story—and they lived happily ever after."

"That wasn't the case. A very frightened Melba showed up on our doorstep nineteen years ago asking for asylum. She answered next to no questions, but requested that she be admitted as a novice. Mother Superior accepted her on a trial basis, and until a year ago she served devotedly. Melba quickly found her niche in records and bookkeeping, doing everything that was expected of her. Everything but one. Throughout all that time, she repeatedly refused to take her final vows, saying she was unworthy."

"So moving on from novice to sister—that's a promotion of sorts?"

Sister Maria Leona stares at me like my question's unworthy of an answer, so I don't press her. Her whole expression turns dark when she continues.

"All last year Melba was spending more and more time away from the convent. In fact, she shocked me by suddenly taking an apartment in town. Shortly afterward, she began acting paranoid, and her health started to fail as well. A few days ago, she finally came clean and confessed everything to me."

I see that Sister's having trouble holding back tears. Turns out, about twenty years ago, in a fit of insanity, Melba stole a whole chunk of money from the Vegas mob—more than 280 big ones— and stowed it away in one of the local bank vaults. The whole time Sister's anonymous sister was hiding out as a novice in the convent, she kept her vow of poverty and never used a penny of the stash for herself. Being in the convent, it was like she gave herself a new identity, no Social Security number needed. The mob couldn't find her under her religious name. Having a great place to hide, Melba lost her fear of the mob and essentially put the stash out of mind, except to keep up the payments on the bank's safety deposit box.

"Whew!" I whistle. "That's some story. So what happened a year ago? Eighteen years is a long time to break a habit... er... no pun intended."

Sister Maria Leone lets out a long sigh and explains. "Melba got to thinking—after all this time, that money wasn't doing anyone any good, so she withdrew the whole stash from the vault and placed it with a stockbroker. She intended to do charitable work with all the interest and dividends the principal had accumulated. She had found religion in a serious way and wanted to accomplish some good with the gains."

I'm getting warmed up to this, concocting my own scenario. "Ah," I break in. "Kind of like Yom Kippur, Melba's atoning, making amends." I steam-roller ahead, guessing instead of listening to the whole story. "So what's going on? Melba's having trouble living with the guilt? You want me to help her return the money to the mob, but she doesn't know how or where or to who? Was there a particular individual injured most by the theft? Is he still around? Does the mob have an accounts receivable department? If they do, how do we avoid their over-anxious, muscled persuaders? Do we leave the cash on the doorstep with a note to take good care of it?"

Sister listens intently, but she looks a little flattened out, then shakes her head. "I wish it were that easy. You see, Melba made a huge mistake. She used her own name, address, and Social Security number on the brokerage account where she deposited the money. As luck would have it, some low-level creep in the firm's accounting office recognized her name from the old days and reported the sighting to a person named Vincente DeNaro."

I like Sister's choice of words. Creep is right. DeNaro is known in loan shark circles as Vinny-the-Viper. Sister tells me he lost no time in paying Melba a threatening visit at her apartment. When she offered to give all the money back, he demanded not only the principal by this coming Friday, but twenty percent interest for each of the twenty years she kept the money. He promised to extract a fingernail for each Friday interest payment she misses. Numerous other painful threats were mentioned in passing.

Sister Maria Leone covers her eyes with her hands and slumps for a moment before straightening up and finishing the sad story. "It's already Wednesday. She only has two days till he comes to collect. I told Melba to return the mob's money to Vincente. After all it's rightfully theirs. But with twenty percent interest for every year? It's impossible. We don't know what to do. I beg you to help us, Slim."

I hate to admit it, but Sister is calling in an old debt. In high school she wrote an English paper on *Hamlet* for me. I got an A, which boosted my C average pretty good. So helping her now is a debt of honor. I don't know exactly what I can do for her, but I sure can't refuse. It's a part of the old neighborhood code.

I agree to go with her to Melba's apartment over on State Street near Elm that afternoon. We grab a taxi. It's about an eight dollar cab fare. But when I reach into my pocket for it, I come up with only six bucks in my Bar Mitzvah money clip and thirty-seven cents in change. Silly, I mean Sister, sees my dilemma, digs into her denim purse, and comes up with enough for both the fare and tip. I grin sheepishly and tell her I'll deduct it from my expenses.

"Don't you carry a credit card?" she asks.

"I accepted one of them new credit cards once—free with no strings attached. A month later I get a letter telling me I'm supposed to enroll in their card protection program for some arm-and-a-leg fee. I wait a few weeks, and when I finally call up to enroll, they tell me it's too late. My identity has already been compromised. So now I got to wonder who I am."

She scowls like she can't figure out if I'm serious or what. We get to Melba's door and Sister knocks. No answer. She calls through the door, and I try my knuckles at pounding. The only result is a neighbor across the hall yelling, "Keep it down out there!"

"You got a key?" I ask her. She shakes her head.

I pull out my universal key set and tickle the lock 'til it opens. I let the door swing back slowly and silently on its hinges. The room is totally dark, so I use the back of my key case to flip the light switch on my right. The suddenly bright living room reveals a starkness to the max. A small rug, a few sticks of furniture, several religious icons. I tell Sister to wait in the hall while I check out the remaining rooms: a tiny kitchen and bedroom with a made-up twin bed in one corner and a table in another.

"There's no sign of Melba," I call over my shoulder, only to find that Sister has followed me in. In a lower voice I suggest, "Couldn't Melba be out shopping or something?"

"I don't think so," Sister replies. "Melba promised to wait until I got here. She usually doesn't break her word. Well, not always, anyway."

Looking around the bedroom once more, I pick up the tiny red glow of an indicator lamp on an electric typewriter. I see there's a sheet of paper left in the machine with two lines of typing on it. At first glance I see:

" J-R-:-{@ B-o-m-v-r-m-y-r F-r-m-s-t-r y-p-p-l <-p n-s-v-l y-p V-r-h-s-a. "

I decide the typing is nothing but gibberish. But then I notice that two of the keys are covered with masking tape and clickity-click, things fall into place.

"You said Melba's health was failing. How was she affected?"

"She has trouble breathing—it's a respiratory disorder."

"Nothing to do with her eyes?"

"Why, yes," Sister replied. "Melba has a severe case of macular degeneration. Even with glasses she can barely see the end of her nose. But how did you know that, Slim?"

"The pieces of tape on the keyboard are usually used to orient a blind typist."

"So, what about it?"

I leave the paper in the typewriter, reexamine the text, and make some notes, Then I announce, "I can read this. She's been kidnapped. DeNaro has taken her back to Vegas, and with this piece of evidence, we've got Mr. Vinny-the-Viper dead-to-rights. Maybe it's time to call in the Feds."

"I wish you wouldn't use that dead-to-rights expression in connection with Melba," Sister responds. "Perhaps we can convince Vinny it's in his best interests to let Melba go. As you say, we do have something on the man."

Sister insists that we confront Vinny immediately, so against all my professional scruples, I agree to go to Vegas with her. When I tell her my jalopy is in hock at the parking lot for lack of fee payments, she offers to pay all the arrears, even though they're worth more than the car.

So eight-and-a-half hours later, we pull up to the valet parking kiosk at the Millennium Gross Hotel. It takes a whole lot of Sister's convincing for them to accept my dilapidated wheels in their fancy lot. Without her nun's headdress, we'd be out on the street. Inside the flashy red and gold lounge, Sister asks for Mr. DeNaro, and this thug, acting like a secretary, tells us to wait, his boss is otherwise occupied. Like we're getting an audience with the Pope.

"Be right back," I tell Sister. She raises her eyebrows 'til they almost touch her bangs. I pretend I don't notice and wander out of the lounge into the casino—a room about the size of Rhode Island. I gravitate to the roulette wheel, which, I kid you not, is hypnotizing. I follow the little ball round and round 'til I get dizzy. It's worse than watching a Ping-Pong match from the fifty yard line. Also, I gotta remember not to lean on the felt playing surface on account of I got this allergy. I break out all over with bee hives, and Vo won't help me apply the calamine lotion where I can't reach. I don't suppose I can ask Sister either—she's got her ethics to watch. This ain't my first visit to Sin City, but I figure if I'm traveling with a nun, what could happen?

They tell me you gotta have a system to make any money at gambling. On a previous visit my ex-brother-in-law, Elmer, introduced me to a foolproof system he learned from one of them croupier guys. Well, my own system was bad enough, but with Elmer's, I lost everything even faster. I should never trust a guy that uses a rake to pull in suckers' money. When I reach into my pocket for a handkerchief, I feel a firm hand on my shoulder. I shoulda known Sister would follow me in. She thinks I'm succumbing to temptation and leads me back to the lounge.

"Not to worry," I assure her as I retrieve the paltry buck-two-ninety-eight from my pocket and show it to her. She smiles and pushes me down into a gilded chair. The door to DeNaro's office opens. The thug secretary comes out with a blank check for five hundred simoleons and hands it to Sister.

"I didn't come here to beg for money," she exclaims as she refuses the check. "I came to see your boss and I'm not leaving until I do."

"Hey, Mr. DeNaro is a very busy man. He don't see no one without an appointment."

He didn't bargain on a nun being one tough cookie. Sister finger-thumps him on his chest, pushes him out of her way, and marches into the office.

"Hey, you can't go in…"

The door slams in his face before he can finish. The thug tries to follow her, and that's when I step between him and the door. "You don't want to mess with Sister. It'd be like disrupting divine intervention and that's like some kind of sin, Mac." I slip into the office behind Sister and close the door.

The large man standing behind the teak desk shouts at us. "Who are you two and what's the meaning of barging into my office?"

Sister glares at him. "Mr. Vinny-the-Viper, you can talk to us or to the Feds. I don't care which, but you are going to talk,"

"Talk? Talk about what? I gave you a check. What more do you want?"

"I didn't come here for a check. I want my sister Melba back—my blood relative, Melba McElvee."

"What the devil you talking about, Sister?"

At this point I step up to the plate and call the man a bald-faced liar. When Vinny starts to reach into the top drawer he's been slowly opening, I reach across the desk and slam it shut on his fingers. He lets out a yelp, retrieves his fingers, and sucks on the bruised knuckles.

"A little respect for Sister Maria Leona! Where's Melba McElvee?"

"I don't have her," he mutters, still rubbing his knuckles.

"You kidnapped her from her apartment last night, and we can prove it," I say.

"Prove it?" he says, "How?"

"She left a message on the typewriter incriminating you."

"Hey, that's nothing but gibberish," he counters. Then he realizes his mistake. "Hey, your word against mine."

"Possibly," I reply. "You may or may not remember the two pieces of tape on the keyboard."

"I don't, but so what?"

"Those pieces of tape on the keyboard are used to orient a blind typist," I tell him. "My Aunt Sophie had diabetic retinopathy and lost her sight as a result of ignoring her diabetes. She used the same method on her old Royal typewriter."

I unfold a sheet of paper and show him my notes on Melba's typing: two lines of gibberish characters and a third line of readable characters below them. While I agree that Melba's characters don't make no sense at all, substituting one keyboard character to the left of the gibberish characters produces the third line of clearly incriminating text:

" J-R-:-{-@ B-o-m-v-r-m-y-r F-s-M-s-t-p y-p-p-l <-r n-s-v-l y-p B-r-h-s-d "

" K-T-"-{-# N-p-,-b-t-,-u-t G-d-<-d-y-[u-[-[-; .-t m-d-b-; u-[N-t-j-d-f"

" H-E-L-P-! V-i--n--c-e-n--t-e D-a-N-a-r-o t-o-o-k m-e b-a-c-k t-o V-e-g-a-s. "

"Hell, that's in your handwriting, and without Melba, no

one's gonna believe you," Vinny shoots back.

"Supposing I tell you that the original is locked up securely back at the convent for a long time, and unless you return Melba immediately, you're going to be locked up for an even longer time. Her fingerprints are the only ones on the paper."

Sister realizes I'm pushing the truth a bit, but knows it's all in a good cause. She nods.

"And if I release her?" Vinny asks.

"Only God and Sister know why, but Sister will return the money—that is, without any interest."

"What about Melba's typed note?"

"We keep that for insurance in case you ever decide to make a move against the McElvee sisters again."

Vinny presses the intercom button and calls his goon into the office. They exchange a few words, then Vinny turns to Sister and me. "I'll have Melba here in twenty minutes. You both can wait out in the lounge."

"What about the five hundred dollar check?" Sister asks.

"Keep it," he says. "I'll deduct it as a charity expense."

Twenty-five minutes later, we have a happy reunion and head back home. All in all, it turns out to be a profitable two days. I take in eleven hundred bucks, and we break sort of even on expenses. But considering the arrears on my parking and the fact that Sister picked up all the tabs, I'm way ahead of the game. Oh, yeah, Slim and Nun still meet at Starbuckets for coffee every now and then.

#

Story Five

Slim Down

THE CLOCK GOT OUT OF HAND and daylight chased after it. I'm grabbing forty winks over my desk with my noggin resting on crossed arms. I'm jolted awake. In the dark an eerie feeling seizes my spine.

I look up just as the office door creaks, then swings open. A shaft of hallway light illuminates a sleek torso, fitted into a silvery sheath like a piece snug in its holster. Ivory stiletto heels gleam in the light like pearl handles. The garish light casts a long shadow that moves closer, evolving into a feminine shape. A round of hip rotates into place with every sensual step. I flick on the desk lamp. My visitor advances with a resolute stride, her head at a belligerent tilt. She speaks—not in your typical sentences, but in sharp, armor-piercing bursts.

"You the private eye?"

"Slim O. Wittz, Private Investigations. Neat, Complete and Discreet, at your service, ma'am." I try to smile, but it comes across more like a grimace.

Her wise-ass reading of my weak professional situation annoys me, so I answer, "No, I don't have a case of the measles or flu."

"You know what I mean."

"I've got a few cases," I lie.

Her dark angry eyes aim down on me from a round Asian face, barreled in by a perfect cap of jet-black hair. No makeup, which gives her a sincere no-nonsense appeal. "Got one now," she fires at me while slipping into my client chair.

"I'll have to check my day book, ma'am, and see if I can fit you into my busy schedule."

"No need," she shoots back. Then, after reloading, "You will take my case."

I'm thinking this dame don't take no for an answer, so I stop with the dumb busy charade and tell her, "I get two-hundred smackers a day plus expenses."

"Agreed." She pops just a crack of a smile.

"Now then, how can I help you, Miss uh…?"

"Cheung, Bunny Cheung. It's about my brother, Lee."

"And what about your brother, Miss Cheung?"

"He's dead. They found him this morning with 200 pounds of barbell across his windpipe. Strangled or crushed, I don't know which. They said it was an accident—he shouldn't have been pushing iron without someone spotting for him. The police agreed quickly, too quickly."

"Who are the *they* you mentioned and where did this take place?" I ask.

"Sam Briar, one of the damn trainers at Bold's Gym, found Lee when he opened the place at 5:45 this morning, The detective thinks it must have happened some time last evening."

"What makes you think his death wasn't accidental, Miss Cheung?"

"My friends call me Bunny, Mr. Slim."

"Sure, Bunny."

"Lee has been using Bold's for years and knows all the rules. First, he wouldn't have been pushing iron without a spotter. Second, a week ago he bragged to me that he'd reached 170 pounds. Two-ten, that's way too big a leap in one week."

"What makes everyone so sure he didn't have a spotter?"

"They all said so." Her voice softens, and a lone tear hangs from feathery lashes. She makes no move to wipe it away, and that ploy bugs me, pulling the helpless damsel thing. But I do have to agree with her about too much of a barbell weight jump, and I wonder why the police eliminated the possibility of murder so quickly. Something smells bad here and it ain't all gym sweat. I'm convinced enough that I'll have to go there and sniff around some for myself. I get her to put her Jane Henry on my standard contract and we shake hands. She gives me the address of the gym, and I tell her I'll start first thing in the morning.

Morning arrives with all the neck cricks and backaches from sleeping on the office Castro Convertible. You see, I'm saving on rent these days and living where I work. I don't need a nerve-jangling alarm clock, because the Café Patisserie on the ground floor sends a waft of heaven to my second floor office at precisely six a.m. every morning.

Vo picks up blueberry muffins and cheese Danish there. Her real name is Voluptuous, but if I call her that, she starts throwing things at me. "Just Vo!" is the way she puts it, even though the doll does fit that name to a tee. She's one-quarter secretary, three-quarters lawyer and a hundred percent smart. Vo speaks legalese all the time now. That's because the dame goes to law school classes three nights a week. It's like having a built-in councilor on my staff. Officially, she doesn't do coffee, windows, or any of those menial tasks, but she breaks the coffee rule when we have breakfast each morning.

I've got a clean shave and a fresh shirt on by the time Vo shows up at eight. I push some paperwork aside so she can set breakfast down on a corner of my desk.

"We've got a case, girl," I announce proudly, raising my extra-large Styrofoam coffee cup to touch hers. A paying case—I start this morning." She's pleased, as this means she'll have a paycheck this month. By the time I finish explaining the case, there's nothing left but crumbs, which I brush into my palm and toss back into my mouth. I take the last swig of joe, swish it around in my mouth and swallow. I'm in a good mood, so I kiss the top of Vo's head quickly and move toward the door.

"Try that again, Mr. Slim O. Wittz and I'll start harassment proceedings."

I have to turn back to face her to see that she's kidding me. She's grinning from dimple to dimple.

I keep my car in a lot two blocks from the office. Well, that's not exactly right. In reality, Fish-Face Eddie keeps my '93 Buick Regal hostage two blocks from the office. That's because I still owe the larcenous pit bull three months back rent. He enforces the holdout with an eighteen-inch tire iron and a nasty grin that breaks into a sneer. Vo worked out an arrangement with this gonif whereby I get to rent back my own car at five dollars an hour with the first hour paid in advance. It's still cheaper than a taxi. Four wrinkled ones and some assorted change later that includes ten pennies, I get behind the wheel. The driver's side door handle is busted. Trying to keep the door shut with my elbow hanging out the open window is something of an art. So I loop the front and rear door handles together with a granddaddy of a rubber band. All set, I turn the key. After some choice words coaxing the engine to turn over, I drive across town to one of the newer strip malls and park in front of Bold's Gym on Kennedy Avenue. My first reconnoitering tells me this sweat factory occupies three storefronts in the mall.

As soon as I let go of the noiseless glass door to Bold's Gym, I see a fetching blonde receptionist busy at her desk I'm thinking she isn't paying attention to me, so I try slipping past into the gym itself.

"Just one minute, buster," she calls out like a booming master sergeant. She doesn't look so cute anymore. "Let's see your membership card."

"I don't have one. I just wanted to speak to a friend of mine in there."

"Sorry, the gym is for members only. It's that privacy thing, you know."

"How do I go about becoming a member?" I ask in a somewhat timid voice.

"You'll have to fill out one of these forms and then be interviewed by one of the trainers," she declares in a less imposing tone, sweetness added, too. I take the form to a chair with a built-in desk and hastily scribble the first thing that comes into my noggin in each of the blocks. I use a phony name, address, and cell phone number. Roughly ten minutes later she takes the form back and scans it. "And just how do you want to pay, Mr. Johnson?"

"You can bill me monthly at that address." Good luck on that, I tell myself.

Suddenly, a smile dances across her face. She picks up the phone and stabs a few buttons on the base. "Hey, Charlie. We got a new customer out here who needs to be interviewed. Andy's available? Wait! The customer's trying to get my attention."

I stop my wild waving to tell her a friend of mine recommended Sam Briar. "Is there any chance I might have my interview with Sam?" She nods and passes my request along to Charlie. A minute or two pass, and I receive a thumbs up.

With my eyeballs glued to a pair of lovely gams and a caboose that snaps to and fro, I follow the blonde through the gym to a nearby office. I always tail a good-looking dame that way. Yeah, it's one of those expertises you pick up as a private eye. A pirouette later, she's gone.

A shirtless Sam in gym shorts rises from his swivel chair and greets me with a pile-driving handshake and loudness fit for the hearing-impaired. "Hi, Philip Johnson. (That's my new moniker.) Welcome to Bold's Gym." He's a six-foot-three Adonis with biceps the size of prize hams and metallic-looking abs.

We sit while he peruses my application. Then he asks me to stand up while he examines all my excessive pudginess. Poking here and pinching there, he asks who it was that recommended him.

"Lee Cheung," I tell him just as he reaches my spare tire. "Ow, that hurts. Take it easy," I complain.

He picks up my application again like he's studying it, stalling for time. "How do you know Lee Cheung?" he finally asks.

"I used to date his sister, Bunny Cheung."

He raises one bushy eyebrow. "You mean Dragon Lady?"

"Not when you get to know her. She's really sweet." I have this policy of defending all my clients.

"You're too damned old and fat for the looks of her."

"Hey!" I bark. "You gonna stand there and insult me or you gonna help me build some muscle?"

"Sorry about that. All the excitement here yesterday, I haven't gotten over it. How tall are you and how much do you weigh?"

"Five-eleven, two-twenty-three," I respond, shaving the weight by twenty pounds and boosting the height by an inch. He jots down the figures. "What kind of excitement are you talking about?" I ask.

"You mean you haven't heard?"

"Heard what?"

"About Lee Cheung, one of our clients," Sam says, as if I'm the world's biggest dummy.

"What about him?"

"He's dead. Poor guy dropped a barbell on himself and suffocated. We had the medics and the police here most of the day. Quite a commotion—I went home with a gigantic headache."

"Good grief," I exclaim, putting on my best surprise mask. "I gotta call Bunny as soon as I leave here. She must be a total mess over this."

"Yeah, she is. I talked to her this morning to offer my sincere condolences."

"When did the accident occur?"

"Must have been night before last, just before closing," Sam replies. "Ten-thirty maybe."

"Wow! And no one discovered him until the next morning?"

"I was the first one in, so I found him. Guess we unknowingly locked him in the building."

"We?" I ask.

"Yeah, Charlie Hess, the manager, and Andy Pike and myself. Charlie went around and turned out the lights, and we all left together at eleven as usual. As far as I knew, everyone else had left at ten forty-five."

Sam Briar gives me another once-over. I think for sure I've asked too many questions and blown my cover. I got that wrong because he pokes me in the gut one more time and says, "Phil, you need a major renovation job. When can you start?"

"Right away, I guess. I'll need to pick up some shorts, sneakers, and a T-shirt."

Sam flips open a large book and runs his fingers across the page, "Andy has some time at one-thirty this afternoon. Can you handle that?"

"Sure!" I reply, trying to act enthusiastic. "I'm thinking I want to get a closer look at the gym and its equipment, especially the weight-lifting station where Lee died."

"Andy will work out a schedule from there." Sam shakes my hand, and on my way out, I catch another exceptional glimpse of the blonde receptionist—she's working the bottom drawer of the file cabinet this time.

Sitting behind the wheel of the Buick once more, I decide to check in at the office. I flip open my cell phone and tap in the necessary numbers. Vo answers in her sexiest voice, "Slim O. Wittz, Private Investigations. Neat, Complete and Discreet. Can I help you?" It sends chills down my spine the way she does that.

"Hi, Vo. It's me. Any calls?"

"Yes. Your ex-brother-in-law, Elmer, called a few minutes ago and said it was urgent."

Oh, no! Not again. Urgent to Elmer means he's found another way to make a quick buck off me.

"Thanks, Vo, see you later."

I remember the time when Elmer tried to sell me shares in a freight car full of bananas and another when he wanted to unload a gross of fake Rolexes. Turned out they didn't have batteries—or innards at all. Just numbers painted on the watch faces. I'm about to close the phone when my curiosity hits me up the side of the head. I strike the numbers on the keypad and wait through two ring tones of "My Dog Has Fleas."

Elmer picks up. "Elmer Platz's house. Elmer ain't here right now. Can I take a message?"

"Cut the crap, Elmer, it's Slim. Pick up, I know it's you. What's so urgent this time?"

"Oh. Hi, Slim," he responds in out-of-breath words. "I know where I can lay my hands on a great buy. Hardly used Kevlar vests, but ya gotta act fast, 'cause they're selling like hot cakes. It might be just the thing for you, Slim. You being a private eye and all."

"It's nice of you to think of me, Elmer. But used? What do you mean used?"

"Hardly at all. There's a few small holes where they pulled slugs out, but you'd never notice if you weren't looking for them. The ones with the holes clean through you can cover up with black electrical tape and nobody would ever know the difference. And don't worry about the fit—one size fits all."

After a long disgusted silence, I answer, "Thanks, Elmer, but I'm short on cash right now."

"I'll take your IOU, good buddy."

"I'll pass. See you around." I flip the phone shut and start the car.

It's one-twenty that same afternoon when I finish changing into my workout clothes in the Bold's Gym locker room. There's a full-length mirror on the door, so I grab a quick gander before stepping out into the gym. At first, I see my expansive gut hanging out in space, so I suck it in defensively. Then I recoil at the hairy legs and knobby knees the guy in the mirror has. I figure there's nothing I can do about them, so I push through the door to the gym proper. I'm immediately struck by the row-on-row of machines just waiting to torture and devour me. I wonder what happens to all the excess fat people lose working out on them. Does it lie on the floor until the cleaning lady comes through with her vacuum cleaner? Is there a market for used fat?

Andy remains in the office until he sees me. "Hiya, Phil, Andy Pike here." His friendly pat on the back sends me three feet forward before I come to an awkward halt. He's broad-shouldered, shorter than I expect, black hair with streaks of gray, and has this little round beard sticking out from his chin.

"Let's start you on the stationary bike and we'll see what you can do."

Andy has to lower the seat before I can even mount the one-wheeled monster. Even then, he has to do it once more so my feet can reach the pedals. I try to push down with my left foot, but the pedal doesn't budge.

"Adjust the loading," he tells me.

The digital readout is "Nine," so I turn the LOAD knob clockwise. I still can't move the damn thing. The readout now shows "Ten." Andy clears his throat, and I turn the knob the other way. The pedal barely budges at "Five," so I continue to "Three" and find I can actually move the pedals there.

"I hear you had quite a lot of excitement here yesterday," I say, trying to sound about as casual as a weightlifter's grunt in these environs.

"Yup."

"Did ya know the guy?"

"Yup."

"Were you his trainer?"

"Yup."

"Did you work with him that day?"

"Some."

"Was it near closing time that night? Were you the last person to see the guy alive?"

"Could be." Andy begins flexing his shoulders and elbows.

Not in any threatening way. More out of nervousness, I think.

"What time was that?"

"You shore do ask a lot of questions, Phil. Who or what are you, man?"

"Just your usual rubbernecker at an accident scene," I say. "Now don't you get your junk in an uproar. I don't mean nothing." The odometer says I've already covered an eighth of a mile, and my knees confirm it. I fail to read Andy's newly acquired, squint-like expression and I'm getting the feeling I'm on dangerous ground 'cause my nape hairs are tingling.

"Look, why don't I try the treadmill now," I offer, attempting to change the subject. I straddle the moving rubber mat while Andy sets the speed to a crawl. Once on board the mill, my feet acclimate to a longish stride. Every few minutes he kicks it up a notch until I'm stumbling somewhere between a horse trot and half-run.

"You a cop? Why are you here?" Andy asks.

Our roles have switched—he's the one asking the questions now. I'm wondering how much faster this contraption can go before I fall on my keester and shoot out the back end.

"No, not a cop." Huff, huff and puff. "I'm a private shamus investigating Cheung's death." Huff, huff and another puff. I don't know how much more of this I can take. The sweat is dripping off my head and down my face. From stress or exercise, take your pick.

"Who's your client, chump?" Andy's mouth is fixed in a grin, but his eyes are cold as an iron barbell.

"Can't tell you." Huff and puff. "Wouldn't be ethical. Privacy and all that, you know." I'm looking over my shoulder at him and seeing him reach for the speed control again.

"Wait, wait, the hell with ethics. It's Bunny Cheung, Lee's sister."

Andy cuts the speed by half and glares. "Why me? Why all the questions for me? I don't have anything to do with the two of them."

I straddle the moving mat once more and stand on the stationary rim before dismounting the run-away treadmill. "Them, you said, *with the two of them*. Who did you mean, Andy?"

"More questions? Haven't you learned your lesson yet?"

"Whoa! Sorry about the hard-nose, but this is the way I make my living."

"Charlie Hess is—I mean was—Lee Cheung's bookie, and this Cheung guy was into him in a big way. You'd get much better answers from Hess. He's over in the weight room now, just finishing with a client."

Finishing *with* a client? Or finishing him period? I don't really want to hear the answer. I pass the bulked-up client, who's just leaving as I enter the weight room. I see yellow police crime tape wrapped around the weight bench next to the light switch. Hess looks up from some paperwork at the adjacent bench. "Hey, aren't you the new client, Johnson?"

"Yeah, Phil Johnson. I'm looking for some beginner tips on bench pressing."

"Well, isn't that a coincidence? I'm a bench press expert. Charlie Hess at your service."

Hess is as broad as he is tall, with chiseled muscles attached to rippling muscle all over his body. Even his face bears that sculpted look. Sweat shines on everything from his balding hairline down to the thick black curls on his chest.

"Isn't it customary for a trainer to assist someone lying on their back bench pressing? I think they call it spotting," I say in my most unschooled voice.

"You got that right," he answers.

"Maybe you could demonstrate the proper way to position yourself on the bench so I can receive the bar without hurting myself."

Hess complies, pulling on a pair of black lifter gloves and stretching out on the bench before me. There are two fifty-pound disks and one ten-pounder on each end of the barbell—220 in all, resting in the cradle above his head.

"Is that too much?" I ask, gesturing at the collection of weights on the bar.

"Oh, no!" he answers. "I can do that easily." His open gloves grip the bar, and I help to lift the collection off the cradle. He lowers the weights to his chest and slowly executes five complete presses, blowing air each time, and then attempts to put the bar back in the cradle.

As he gets close to the cradle, I nudge the bar away, so he must continue to either support the total weight or lower it to his chest. Four grunting tries and four wave-offs later, he's convinced I'm not your ordinary client.

I take my cue from his hard breathing. "Why'd you kill Lee Cheung, Charlie?"

"You're crazy, Phil, or whatever your real name is."

"The name is Slim O. Wittz and I'm a private investigator looking into Cheung's murder."

"You're gonna have a hell of a time proving that lie," he gasps out.

"It's no lie, Charlie, and I can prove it."

"Oh yeah? How?"

"Lee was alive at ten-thirty when Andy last saw him. If he was alive at eleven when the lights went out, don't you think he would have complained, shouted or something? Besides, you couldn't have missed him stretched out on the bench right next to the light switch."

"Andy could be mistaken or lying. He could have done it."

Charlie Hess makes another grunting attempt for the cradle, and I push it away. I pull a couple of rubber exercise bands from the wall and tie his legs to the bench so he can't roll off. I know it'll be awhile before he tries again. I also add another twenty-five pounds to each side, and he lets out the yell from hell when his elbows buckle and shoulder cracks.

"Okay, okay, I did it. Get this friggin' weight off of me. My right shoulder and rotator cuff are busted. It was an accident, but it didn't go down like it looked."

"I'm listening," I say. Sam and Andy are also listening as they burst through the weight room doorway in response to Charlie's yell.

"I didn't set out to kill him. I didn't mean to." Tears welled up in Charlie's eyes. "I only wanted to scare him into paying something on his gambling debt. He owed me over $8,000 and kept putting me off to the next week, and the next week, on and on. Like I can carry that much in my small book operation. I held the bar over his head as if I was gonna drop it. Only he grabbed my hand, and I accidentally let go. The bar did hit him across the windpipe."

I shout to Sam and Andy, "You guys watch him while I call the police. Remember what you just heard and witnessed."

I fish my cell phone out of the gym locker and call Vo. She, in turn, calls the law and my client. Then the whole kaboodle shows up at the crime scene. The two trainers release Hess from my heavy-handed workmanship, and the police take him into custody.

Satisfied, Bunny writes me a healthy check, and Vo takes it into custody. I endorse it. She'll actually get paid this month. How will I eat and pay my rent? That's easy. I'll borrow part of it back from her.

#

Story Six

Slim Pickings

I'M SLIM O. WITTZ, a private investigator. Wait! Private eyes are people, too. We're called shamuses, techs, Peeping Toms, and snoopers. Despite all the name calling, we serve an important need in the mix of things. It's kind of a tough living, and making our ends meet sometimes calls for creative planning. I hate to admit it, but I live in my office, and my car is in one of those purchase-and-leaseback deals like the airlines. I pay by the hour to rent my own car. Yeah, I know, it ain't ideal.

Vo's at her desk typing away on one of her law school papers. The dame's quite a looker—decorates the office with her clingy sweaters and short skirts, so I don't have to put up pictures. I had to promote her from secretary to paralegal 'cause I couldn't afford to give her a raise.

This is one of those slow months, so I'm taking my afternoon nap, resting my head on my folded arms. Vo's typing doesn't bother me either—it's just slow enough that I can get ten winks of snooze per keystroke. I'm awake now, but I ain't opened my eyes yet. I feel a breeze on the back of my neck. The window facing the brick wall is open on account of Vo just covered the joint in bug spray. She's been complaining for weeks about the roach invasion. I ain't seen one of the nasty invaders yet, but she wants to call an exterminator. I put her off, hoping the beasts will move on to someone else's office.

I slowly roll one lid up and there, right on the desk in front of me, staring into my one open eye is one of the bolder roaches checking me out like I'm something to conquer. Ugh!

"Vo! Call already, get estimates for fumigation."

"No problem, boss," she warbles as she slips out of her chair and glides toward me. She's carrying a sheaf of papers. I shoulda known. She's had the estimates for days. She lays them down in front of me and spins away before I can get a good look at the smirk on her face. Five pest control firms. All of their figures are astrological, way off in the future, even. Each estimate is more than we've netted for the past three months.

It's time I exerted my authority. "There's got to be another way!" I pound the desk with my fist. It hurts like hell. "My ex-brother-in-law, Elmer, maybe?"

"No way, Jose!" Vo retorts. Her voice carries a tremor of fear.

"Well, Elmer does know how to get things cheap. He scrounged up those reversible sport coats for fifteen bucks apiece. And remember the no-rub spot remover? Only a buck-fifty a can."

"Wasn't that the stuff that melted the buttons on my red dress?"

"It got the spot out, didn't it?"

"Yeah, Slim, but I sure won't be the one dealing with that dirtbag. You'll have to do it."

I punch in the numbers to his land line, and after four rings, the answering machine takes over. "Pick up, Elmer," I shout into the phone. "It's Slim, not one of your pit-bull creditors. You're safe."

"Hi, Slim," he begins. "I hope you're not still mad at me over the Dockers knockoffs. How was I to know the seam threads weren't knotted?"

"Elmer, that's polluted water over the dam. I need something else—someone to fumigate the office. Do you know anyone in the business?" I can hear pages turning.

"Have I got a deal for you." It's his Karo syrup M.O. in action.

"Never mind the deal, Elmer. How about giving me his phone number?"

"That's the problem—he doesn't have one."

Oy! That's just what I need, a fly-by-night, a spritz-and-run.

"I'll have him call you, and you can make your own appointment." He hangs up before I can say no.

A half-hour later the phone rings, and Vo sings her way through our standard reply. "Slim O. Wittz, Private Investigations. Neat, complete and discreet." She turns to me. "It's for you, Slim."

I pick up on my extension and ask, "Who am I talking to?"

The voice rasps, "It's Yasha Rosen from Rosen Ex…terminators." He squeezes it out like he's no longer in the business.

"Are you an experienced firm with all the necessary equipment?"

"Sure, I got experience. Can't you tell? I'm not a young man anymore."

I see Vo trying to get my attention and put my hand over the mouthpiece. "What?" I ask.

"See if his firm is bonded."

"Are you bonded?" I ask.

"Of course, sonny, I buy Israeli bonds every year."

"How good are you, Mr. Rosen?"

"Vell, my good man, none of the varmints has lived to sue me yet."

I look up at the crack in the ceiling and try again, "How much do you charge?"

"Sixty bucks a room."

The price is right, and I can't think of anything else to ask, so I give him the address. He tells me he can fit me in this afternoon.

A little after one-thirty, Vo hears a soft knock at the door and yells, "Come on in."

The door opens wide, revealing a brisk little man—in his early eighties, I'm guessing. Maybe it's the white bushy head of hair, the roadmap of wrinkles and the soulful blues in half-glasses. Yasha Rosen, dressed in clean bibbed overalls, sets a brown paper grocery bag on the desk and begins removing the tools of his trade. There's a candle, a feather, an unmarked can of powder, and a spritz bottle of what looks like ant and roach killer.

"What're the candle and feather for?" I inquire.

"The good Lord gave me my start looking for hametz —you know, searching for bread and cake crumbs before Passover in Orthodox homes. So you see, I can't part with tradition, sonny, no matter how hard I try."

"What's in the bottle and can?"

Yasha rolls his eyes. "Dyn-a-mite! And if you got any more questions, I'll have to charge you for another room. Don't be a schlemiel, sonny—time is money, you know."

I'm forced to let Yasha do his thing, and surprisingly, the old man gets down on all fours and nimbly covers all the floor moldings with a white powder, then climbs up on a chair and sprays inside all the cabinets. When he finishes, he wipes his hands with a cloth from his back pocket. All his equipment goes back into the grocery bag, and he stands beside my desk, patiently waiting for payment.

"I'm impressed with your effort, Yasha. You can send me a bill."

"Sorry, sonny, it's a cash-and-carry business. I need payment now. Didn't Elmer tell you?"

"Elmer didn't say, and I can't pay 'til after the first of the month. Don't worry, old man, I'm good for it."

"I see," he says, rubbing a knotty hand across his stubbled chin. "Maybe you can work it off, Mr. Wittz."

"Call me Slim, Yasha. How can I work it off? Do you need my investigative services?"

"As a matter of fact, I do. You see, my granddaughter, Reba, has run away, and I haven't heard from her in over a week. She's only sixteen, and I'm all she has. Her parents, they should rest in peace, were killed during a break-in at their home. She slept through the whole thing and then discovered the bodies the next morning. I'm worried about her—she's been through so much."

"How long ago was that terrible trauma?" I ask.

"Four years ago next month."

"Has she adjusted to living with you?"

"I thought so. She's been an absolute dumpling most of the time."

"Have you talked with the police?"

"Yes, but as soon as I told them she was a voluntary runaway and I didn't suspect foul play, they told me they don't have the time or manpower to chase down every runaway in the city."

"How do you know she went voluntarily?" I ask.

"She left me a note on the kitchen table. It said, 'Grandpa, I'm taking a little vacation from everything. Don't worry about me.' Can you believe that? She's supposed to be in school!"

"Do you know why she ran off?" I ask.

"I disapproved of the older boy she was dating. His name is Al Something."

"How much older?"

"He's over twenty, not a college boy, and hasn't got a job."

"You think she moved in with the bum?"

"God forbid! She's been such a good girl. Gets good grades, too." He sighs. "But there's always the possibility."

"Have you talked with any of her girlfriends?"

"Yes, all those that I can remember, but how do I know

whether they were telling me the truth?" He shakes his head. "I thought if I bought her a cell phone she'd stay home and spend her time texting, like other kids do. Boy, was I wrong. It's difficult with girls that age."

Any age, I'm thinking. I fire a few dozen more questions at the old man. "Yasha," I say, "I'll give you a half-day free of charge. Then I gotta charge you two hundred smackers a day plus expenses. It's my regular fee."

"Okay, sonny, but it's a hundred a day for five days max and we'll have a deal."

I look over at Vo, and she's put two thumbs in the air, so I nod, and she types up a contract amendment for Yasha to sign.

"We're forgetting something, Yasha, and it's important. A photo of Reba."

He takes an envelope out of his pocket and hands me her high-school class picture. Beneath curly light brown hair, cut short above her ears, a wan face struggles to strike the class-picture smile. Alert deep blue eyes, very like her grandfather's, peer out from black-framed cat's-eye glasses, quite at odds with her fair complexion.

Ten minutes later, down on the street in front of the office, I promise the old man I'll keep in touch. Armed with Reba's picture, her cell phone number and a list of her friends, I go my way and Yasha goes his.

I check my Buick Regal out of hock, and at the first traffic light, peruse my notes. Al Something is not going to hack it for the boyfriend's name and location, so I move down to the first girlfriend on the list, Lillian Markus. "Lil," as she prefers to be called, won't let me in the house, so I speak to the door. Although I'm quite used to speaking to inanimate objects, I never know when I'm getting through to a door. No, the door doesn't know Reba's whereabouts, nor had it been in touch with her in over a week. The only things I learn at the Markus home is that Al stands for Albert and not Allan or Alfred and definitely no last name. That the guy's cute, but a little on the wimpy side doesn't help me much.

I move on to the next name and address on the list. Monica Leonard, or rather her mother, Beatrice, proves way more hospitable. As soon as I explain why I'm there, Bea ushers me into the parlor, then floats off to the kitchen, hips swaying and torso slinking. She returns, all smiles, carrying a hot tea service and a plate of rugulah, little pastries filled with poppyseed, apple, and nuts. My favorite. Bending to pour directly in front of me, she delivers more than just the tea. I loosen my tie. I get the message, but I'm not buying. She sits across from me. All the while I'm grilling her chubby little Monica, buxom Bea is giving me one wink after another and toying with the buttons on her blouse. Two more buttons come undone. I don't know whether to "Wow!" or "Whoa!" Something about it, or her—Comedy Central maybe.

The daughter doesn't seem to notice or care, but she tries to be helpful. She doesn't know Albert's last name, but she thinks he lives over on Third Street near the CVS Pharmacy and Clinton's Laundry. She heard from Reba a few days after her friend ran away. Monica won't tell me about the exact conversation. "I promised not to," she pleads, but she does jot down a few joints where she's seen Reba and Al hang out. Bea suddenly turns off the vamp act. "What were you doing around there, young lady?"

I'm not eager to hear the answer. Thanking them both, I stand up to leave when Monica's cell phone rings. She checks the number and vacates the room for privacy, leaving me alone with Mom. I wonder whether it's Reba.

"Do you find me attractive?" Bea asks.

Uh-oh, here we go again. "Yes, ma'am," I mutter, my mouth full of apples and poppyseed.

"Mr. Leonard used to say he found me h-h-hot."

I could feel the heat already, so I start edging out of the living room. "I'm sure he did, ma'am."

She leads me into the hall and brakes to a stop—trapping me between her cleavage and the door.

"He couldn't wait to come home nights."

"I can see why, ma'am. And, uh, where is Mr. Leonard?"

"We're divorced," she sniffs. "Not amicably, if you must know." She presses a business card into my hand. Glancing at it, I see that her phone number is printed even larger than her name.

"Call me Bea, Slim. 'Bye now."

Both B's shape her lips into kisses. Don't get me wrong, I like dames a whole lot, but this broad's a steamroller. I slip out the door like a snake doing corners.

Snug in the safety of my Buick, I consider the last girlfriend and address on Yasha's list. Sheila Morris answers the doorbell, and as soon as I explain my mission, invites me into the living room. Her parents are both at work, and I wonder why she allowed me into the house. Sheila is all tears, a box of Kleenex in her lap. A skinny girl with spiked yellow hair and black nail polish, she tells me Reba is her best friend, so she wants to cooperate, but I get the feeling Best Friend is holding something back.

"I feel like a traitor telling you this," she says. The silver ring piercing her lower lip quivers. "But I don't think Albert has her best interests at heart. He's just trying to get into her panties." A surprisingly grown-up comment, followed by, "Wait a sec." She jumps up and darts from the room, returning a moment later with a photograph. "This is from a party we were all at a couple weeks ago."

I recognize the face and hair, but here she's in a tank top with hip-hugger jeans and bare belly. I can pretty well bet her grandfather hasn't seen her in this get-up.

"That's Albert with her," Sheila says. The man looks about twenty-five, and has his arm slung possessively around Reba's shoulders. His dark hair is slicked back in a ponytail. I'd have sworn he'd be wearing a black leather jacket, but we all have to face our disappointments. He's wearing a blue turtleneck.

"Have you heard from her?" I ask.

"Three days ago she texted me," Sheila whimpers, "but all she wrote was that she was okay."

I hear the front door slam shut. A six-foot-plus man who could pass for The Terminator strides into the foyer. His jaw goes slack when he notices that his daughter is blubbering and a strange man has invaded his castle. A purple flush creeps across his face and he begins to bellow.

"What the hell are you doing in my house? What have you done to my daughter?" Before I can answer, he spins around and pulls a baseball bat from the hall closet. Raising the bat in a wide sweep, he takes out the hall chandelier. "Damn!" he shouts, as he ducks the shards of glass showering down on the ceramic tile floor. He hesitates for a moment, then stalks into the living room to do serious damage to me.

"I haven't done anything to your daughter," I plead. "I'm Slim O. Wittz, a private—"

"I don't care if you're the Secret Service. You can't come into my house and assault my daughter." He raises the bat once more.

"No, Daddy, no!" Sheila shouts. "He's investigating Reba's disappearance. He's a private investigator working for Reba's grandfather." She runs between us and into his arms, forcing him to lower the bat. "He's only trying to help her."

Mr. Gregory Morris stops in his tracks and listens for the first time—maybe for the first time in his life. "They haven't found poor Reba yet?" The bat drops to the floor.

"No, Daddy."

"Sorry, Mr. Wittz. I had no way of knowing." Morris offers a hand, and we shake. I'll Ben-Gay my bruised knuckles later. All the while, I'm thinking this S.O.B. is worried that I'll sue the shirt off his back. Which I'd be delighted to do—it'd pay my bills. I tuck the party picture in my pocket, thank the two of them, and tiptoe through the crunching glass on my way out the door. By the time I reach my jalopy, I can feel the rumbling in my stomach; I haven't eaten all day. Besides, I think I've given Yasha a fair half-day of work.

I check the car back in with its keeper and tell Fish-Face Eddie to put it on the tab. He waves a threatening tire iron at me and warns, "First of the month."

"Yeah, Eddie, you get paid when I do." I walk the two

blocks to my office building, but I don't go directly upstairs. Instead, I cross the street and enter the local elegant establishment with its signature aroma of frying fat and two-day-old coffee. All the booths are empty. Two people are seated at the counter and one of them is my bookie, who I owe thirty smackers. I set my tuchas down in a booth with my back to him and hope he doesn't recognize me.

Sourpuss Sally heads my way. Her smile muscles atrophied years ago. If she weren't the owner's wife, she'd be out of a job, for sure. She jams the menu into my gut. I know it by heart, so I don't bother to open it.

"What're the specials tonight?" I ask.

"Same's every Thursday night, Slim—Hungarian goulash and fish and chips."

"Goulash got any veggies?"

"Should I get you a dictionary, Smart Boy? That's what goulash is, meat and vegetables."

"Thanks a lot, Sally, cut the lecture."

"Let's see, we had peas last night, carrots on Tuesday, string beans on Monday, and there's celery and potatoes left over from last week. Can I get you some, Mr. Picky?"

I have no idea what "some" involve. "Sure," I say in a forced cheerful note.

"Anything else?"

"Some rye bread, please."

"No rye, wanna try again?"

"Sourdough?"

"Nope!"

"Pumpernick?"

"Nope!"

"French bagettes?"

"Nope!" Her face remains deadpan, but I can tell she's enjoying this.

"Eyetalian facaccio?"

"Nope!"

"Whole wheat?"

"Nope!"

"Russian health bread?"

"Nope!"

"Got any bread at all?"

"Nope, but we got some stale bran muffins from breakfast."

"I guess I'm stuck with the muffins. Bring me a couple."

"You could have some of them salty bread sticks."

"No. I'll stick with the muffins."

"There's some Saltine crackers from chili, too."

"Cut that out already. I'm having goulash and muffins."

The left side of her mouth curls slightly, suppressing a smirk after annoying me. While I'm waiting, I use the time to check in with Yasha. My report seems to please him. At least it isn't bad news.

Sourpuss Sally arrives with my supper, dropping both plates in front of me like a B-52 bomb. The shrapnel lands a prominent brown spot on my new sport coat, which also serves as my business attire. Without a word, Sally takes the hem of her apron, dips it in my water glass, and wipes it to a lighter shade of tan. I figure that's the extent of her guilt, so I check out the goulash.

"It's watery," I complain. I'm also thinking those crackers would come in handy about now.

"What did ya expect, it's after eight-thirty. The chef tells me, Don't dip so deep—it's got to last 'til nine."

"What would it take to increase the population in my bowl, Sally?"

"Increase my tip to five bucks, and I'll see what I can do. Remember, I ain't no deep sea diver, neither."

A man can't live by love alone, so I agree. Sally picks up the bowl and returns with a plate of solid meat and veggies. Quite tasty, too.

Next morning, I borrow a fin from Vo, leave the sport coat for her to work on the spot, and head downstairs to the fresh carbon monoxide. Third Street ain't so far, so I hoof it on over there. On the way I see one of them office copy places and enlarge the party photo. The first joint on Monica's list is a pool hall. You might think the last bastion of the unemployed would be empty at 10:30 on a weekday morning. No way. A crowd is deeply engaged in a game of snooker. I wisely wait for the break between games before passing around the picture.

"Anyone here know where I can find Albert?" I point to him in the photo.

A pink Mohawk in ripped T-shirt and jeans answers: "Who's the broad? She's hot."

"She's only sixteen," I answer. "You want to go to the slammer for robbing the cradle?" He shakes his head.

A tubby guy with blond hair, black shirt, and chinos says, "What do you want Bad Al for?"

"I owe him some cash," I say. "And I always pay my football bets."

"Cash, I could use some cash, gringo," mimics a mustached Hispanic. He smiles, baring many teeth, one of them black.

The fourth member of the group has a crew cut and sits quietly in a chair, observing the goings-on. I have a feeling he's their leader. I shove the picture in his face. He points his thumb toward the street.

Outside, I hesitate long enough to consult my notes and then begin walking uptown. As I pass the alley between the pool hall and laundry, a large hand grabs my sweatshirt by the collar, yanks me off the sidewalk, and shoves me up against the concrete block wall. When my eyeballs come back into focus, I'm staring at the pink Mohawk. He must have used a side door to get here so quickly. He pulls a switch-blade knife from his pocket and starts tossing it from hand to hand while shifting his weight from foot to foot. It's as if he expects me to take up his challenge. I see that he lacks experience at this sort of thing, as his eyes are following the blade from side to side.

I'm not the bravest mark in the city, but I've learned not

to show fear in this kind of situation. So I start a conversation. "I've been thinking of getting a Mohawk just like that." Surprised, he looks up for a second to see if I'm for real, then monitors the knife-tossing again. I press on. "Who's your barber? He did a great job. Is it the guy over on Oak Street ?" The Mohawk stops shifting his weight and looks up at me again, his face a riot of dimwitted confusion. Then I hear his blood-curdling screech echoing through the alley.

I'm amazed to see the blade of his shiv sticking through the center of his left palm. The knife had turned over in its flight from the right hand. Blood begins to ooze, so I step closer, grab his hand, and pull the blade free. I use my handkerchief to stem the flow and push him along to the street, where I hail a passing cab. By the time I stuff him into the back seat, the klutz is almost catatonic. I give the driver the fin I borrowed from Vo and say, "Get him to the emergency room and step on it." I've always wanted the opportunity to say *step on it*. The cab races off toward the hospital.

The next joint on Monica's list is an Internet cafe at Third and Buchanan. I check the change in my pocket—a buck-ninety-two, just enough for a cup of mud. I plop my tuchas on the only available stool (in my business I seem to do a lot of tuchas plopping). Without asking, the counterman pours out a mug of coffee and shoves all the accoutrements at me.

"Know this guy in the photo?" I ask him.

"Can't you see I'm busy?" he answers.

"Just look. Looking takes only a second."

"Yeah, it's Bad Albert Burstine. He lives upstairs with his old man."

"How do I get up there?" I drop a buck-fifty in quarters on the counter.

"Outside, first door on the right, third floor."

Huffing and puffing, I arrive at the third floor landing and face three unmarked wooden doors. I do an eeny, meeny, miny, moe, knock on the first one, and an old lady in curlers answers.

"Burstine?" I ask. She points to her right. I knock and

wait.

A baby-faced character with a ponytail and egg-shaped body answers. I'm thinking, this guy can't be Bad Albert; the looks don't fit the name, and he can't be twenty yet.

"Is Albert Burstine in?"

"Yeah, I'm Albert. Who are you?"

"I'm Slim O. Wittz, private investigator." I hand him my business card, and when he's through reading, "I'm investigating the disappearance of one Reba Rosen."

He hesitates, then holds the door for me to step in. "So what do you want from me?" he asks.

"Her grandfather is terribly worried about her. He thinks she might be staying here with you."

"I don't know where he got that idea. It's just me and my old man living here." The elder Burstine is in the next room, sitting at the kitchen table, nodding his agreement.

"Stop!" a soprano voice calls out. Reba Rosen suddenly appears behind Albert. "I can't do this anymore. I'm ready to go home. Now."

"You all right, miss? He hasn't mistreated you?"

"I'm fine, and he hasn't harmed me—at all. In fact, he's been wonderful to me, Mister—"

"Wittz, Slim O." Reba hardly looks like her class picture. She's fair-skinned, all right, but her feminine jaw has a strong set to it. She's taller than I imagined, willowy, but with self-assured posture. Her blue eyes meet mine without fear.

I clear my throat. "This is a tough question, but I gotta ask. "Are you two shacking up together?"

"Oh, no, nothing like that." Her tone is indignant. "Al's a gentleman and sleeps on the couch in the living room. He gave me his room."

Albert The Egg takes a step toward me, not at all aggressive, just determined. "You mean you've come to take her home?"

"Of course!" I retort.

Albert pumps his fist in the air. "Yes! It's about time!"

"Huh?" I respond. "What's going on here anyway?"

"This darling little lady? The minute she set foot in my house, she turned into a Jewish mother. *My* mother, may she rest in peace. I haven't had a moment's peace myself since Reba got here. It's 'Take out the garbage.' 'Get the Ajax, your toilet's disgusting.' 'When are you going to clean out your fridge, things are alive in there.' Yakkety yakkety yak. Even my dad's had it."

I turn to Reba, who is looking a mite sheepish. "Grandpa's a neatnik, so I guess I am, too. Having all this freedom isn't exactly what I expected."

By now I'm swimming upstream. I bring out the party photo and hold it up to her. "Are you leading a double life or are you just schizoid?"

Albert chuckles. "You got a bad case of rebellion, didn't you, kid?"

Reba's face turns the color of cranberries. "Yeah. That outfit, that's not the real me. Grandpa would ground me for life if he saw it."

Still confused, I shake my head. "But what're you doing here, young lady?"

Not-so-Bad Albert seems to take pleasure in replying for her. "She wanted to get away for awhile. We're just good friends— we like the same books and music and stuff. I haven't touched her."

"So," I ask him, "if you're such a perfect gentleman, why do they call you Baaad Albert?"

He grins, his baby cheeks turning rounder still. "In this neighborhood you need a title like that to survive. By the way, am I in trouble for helping Reba out?"

"I don't think so," I reply. "Maybe the three of us should go back and have a pow-wow with Grandfather Yasha."

* * *

I get back to the office around four, and Vo is getting ready to leave for the day. She stops combing her platinum pageboy long

73

enough to ask, "So what happened?"

"Yasha was so pleased to see Reba healthy and happy, and to learn that Albert is not only a member of the tribe, but a mensch as well, that he sat down and wrote me a check for two-hundred-fifty simoleans." I take the check from my pocket to show her. She snatches it from my fingers.

"You mean he wrote us a check, don't you?" Vo turns it over and lays it on the desk. "Sign it, please. I'll even give you a receipt," she says with a wicked smile.

As soon as I endorse it, she slips the check into her purse.

"Hey, I gotta live, too!" I protest.

She digs four twenties out of her wallet and hands them to me. "By the way, the parking lot guy called."

I groan. I can count on only three things in my life. Death, taxes, and Fish-Face Eddie.

#

Story Seven

Slim and Trim

"BUON GIORNO, SIGNORE SLIM," the jovial man greets me. The proprietor's mournful voice greets me. Not great for customer relations and not at all like him.

I'm walking into Scalapini's Barbershop across the street from the office. The one-chair shop belongs to Gepetto Scalapini, sort of a Papa Hemingway in appearance, complete with barrel chest and a grizzled facial bush.

Seated in the chair is a little geezer with a snow-white fringe surrounding Bald Mountain. I have to wait my turn. It won't be long now, if you excuse the pun. I mosey over to a row of rattan chairs next to the mirrors, but I know better than to steal a look at myself. Not only do my ears need lowering, but my paunch as well. I'm stuck with my skosh too much nose and too-square Dick Tracy jaw. Still, not all bad for a forty-one-year-old. At least that's what I keep telling myself.

I take off my windbreaker and leather holster and hang them on the clothes tree in the rear where I can keep an eye on things. A Colt .45 automatic sits snugly in the holster. It's inoperable, which means I don't have to worry about someone else getting hold of my piece and creating mayhem with it. So why do I carry a weapon that doesn't work? It's my calling card and sends a pretty obvious message. Don't mess with Slim O. Wittz, Private Investigator. Oh, the piece is registered, all right—as an antique, complete with filed-down firing pin. I get some of my finest business this way, and it's a lot easier than buying business cards.

I'm here in this clip-joint because Vo gave me an ultimatum: she won't loan me any more money 'til I get a haircut or learn guitar and join the Rolling Stones.

The ancient geezer's finished. Gepetto brushes off the chair and shakes out the striped cape before Velcro-ing it behind my neck. I've been bringing my wavy untamed locks here for years—not because he's the best barber, but because he's the cheapest. He's generally a happy and chatty sort with an elephant's knowledge of any sport you'd care to bring up. But today the man is quiet and sluggish. I try to start a conversation several times, but I'm getting one-word responses. He's leaning on my shoulders and pulling hairs, and I'm not so sure the shears are at fault.

"What's wrong, Gepetto?"

"Niente, Signore Slim."

"Come on," I shoot back. "You've never acted like this before. Something's bothering you."

"Pietro, he's a my son." Gepetto lets out a big sigh, and the buzzing on my head halts. "But he likes I call him Peter in American."

"Well, what about Peter? Tell me."

"He's in a big a trouble with the policia." Gepetto sets down the electric clippers and spins the chair around so we are face to face.

"Has the boy been arrested?"

"Si, Signore Slim." His voice chokes as he blinks back

tears.

"On what charge?"

"Murder, but he no kill nobody. Peter swear he don't."

"How old is the boy?"

"Nineteen last March."

"Have you got him a good mouthpiece?"

"I can no afford a lawyer. The arraignment court, she appointed a Mr. Ginzberg from Legal Aid to help him."

Gepetto tells me Peter was bullied into joining a street gang called the Falcons six months ago. Last Thursday these Falcons got into a neighborhood rumble with the Barons, another local gang. Usually, both sides came away severely beaten with bruises, bumps, black eyes, bloodied noses, and a few surface knife slashes. This rumble turned out fiercer than most. Sixteen-year-old Manny-the-Snake was knifed to death. An unconscious Peter was found lying in the gutter with the knife, the murder weapon, in his hand and his shirt soaked in blood. The police believe that Peter was beaten in revenge for committing the murder. They're guessing that the killing was some kind of initiation ritual.

I calm Gepetto down long enough for him to finish my haircut. It's a pretty good job except for one bald spot the size of a fifty-cent piece, where he skinned me when he talked about his son's bloody shirt. He insists on a no-charge haircut. Fingering the landing strip upstairs, I decide to accept his offer.

I walk the two blocks to the parking lot, where my car is in hock up to its dashboard, and notice that lot attendant, Fish-Face Eddie, ain't watching my '93 Buick Regal. In fact, the ball-buster is nowhere in sight. The Buick runs okay, but let's say it's on number eight of its nine lives. The upholstery is wall-to-wall duct tape—in its early days it was leather, and you can see the road through the floor boards. I figure that's a plus with no air conditioning. The once red-and-white paint job is in equal competition with rust. I try to sneak off without Fish-Face Eddie seeing me so I don't have to pay the back rent on my own car at two bucks an hour. I see him in the rear view mirror running out of the port-a-potty, holding on to his pants with one hand and brandishing a tire iron in the other. I'll deal with him later.

I nurse my aging chariot into the street and chug down to the thirteenth precinct, where they're holding the Scalapini kid. He's sitting on a cot, cradling his bandaged head in his hands.

"Hello, Peter."

My voice startles him. He jumps up and I'm face to face with six lanky feet of pure panic, scared dark eyes, and day-old chin scruff. The only way I can interview him is through the cell bars. Peter can't remember anything after the first gang confrontation. He shows me a baseball-size lump on the back of his head that just might be the cause of his memory lapse. There's a round, dark-red stain on the bandage the size of a manhole cover. I ask about the knife.

He protests, holding up his bruised bare knuckles for me to inspect. "I use my fists. I never carry a weapon into rumbles. The shiv ain't mine and I don't know who put it in my hand. Some S.O.B., that's all I know."

I learn that the whole rift is over Manny-the-Snake from the Falcons dating the sister of one Bully Mahone, the Barons gang's boldest, most-feared leader. "What makes this Mahone cat so fearsome?" I ask.

"He's all muscle—big and tall like man-mountain, and he bullies the other Barons into doing everything for him."

Peter knows there's no way his father can put up the kind of bail the court is asking, so he's resigned to cold storage until the trial. I give Pietro una piccolo bit of hope and a couple of Snickers bars I keep in reserve for long stakeouts, and leave the joint.

Sitting in my parked car outside the county hoosegow, I wonder how much the D.A. has on my client. I need specific information to work with. But where to get it?

Time to put in a call to my ex. She's got a new job working in the county prosecutor's office. Fawn and I split amicably because we ain't revocably compatible. She sleeps during the day—I snooze at night. She likes chick flicks—I prefer oaters. Fawn eats weed and seed salads—I don't eat sham food. She wears fancy duds—I'm comfortable in jeans and shorts. Fawn drinks shooters—I guzzle Bud. The only thing we agreed on was sex. You get the idea. Now she's back living with her mom, who just happens to be more my kind of gal. Subtract fifteen years, and I'd marry the older broad in a Slim minute. I flip open my cell phone and stab in the familiar numbers.

"Hi, Mom, howzit?" I gotta ask that, but then I'm forced to listen. When she's finished analyzing the neighborhood and world news and whether I'm getting enough to eat, I ask if Fawn is available. I can hear a squabble in the background through a muffled palm over the mouthpiece: "I'm not here, I don't wanna to talk to him."

Suddenly, Fawn is on the line. "Hello?"

"Hi, Fawn. Hear you have a new job . . . with the county prosecutor's office. A receptionist even. Do ya like it? Uh-huh, nice people, eh?" I make like I'm truly interested, and we chit-chat for a bit before I get down to my real purpose for calling.

"Fawn, I hate to do this, but I need a professional favor."

"What?" she snaps. "I thought you were calling to wish me luck in my new job. Now you're talking favors."

"Whoa, baby! You weren't so shy to ask for a favor when your ex-boyfriend, Pinsky, was punching you around and riding rough on you. I rushed into that like a Boy Scout."

"Some Boy Scout. You went after the wrong guy. You always rush in and mess things up. That's how you screwed up our marriage, you bastard."

I try to calm her down, but she goes on and on about my always stressing her out. I can hear the tears squeezing out all over the phone.

"At least listen to me," I plead. "And if you don't want to help. Just say so… No, not now! Wait 'til I explain. I've got this paying client whose son is awaiting trial for murder. It would help me a lot to know what your boss has on him. All I need is a quick look at the boy's file."

Her shrieks of anger assault my ears and, for that matter, the entire telephone system. "You mean the evidence. I can't do that. You're not even his attorney. My boss would fire me if I released that kind of information. It might even blow Mr. Browning's case and cost him a win. I won't have anything to do with it."

"But what if the kid's innocent?" I protest.

"You can't know that until you see all the evidence, can you?"

I can't come up with an answer for that one, so I thank her for listening and ask her to put Mom back on the line.

"Oh, no, I'm wise to you, Mr. Slim O. Wittz," Fawn fires back. "You want to get Mom to twist my arm. You think I didn't learn anything in the three-year circus we called a marriage?" She ends the tirade with a Bronx cheer and hangs up on me.

I close the phone and try to think of my next move. At least I got Fawn to spill the beans on who is handling the case. I'd still like to know what ADA Howard E. Browning has on my client, but that will have to wait for now. He insists that everyone call him Howie! To hear him say it—it sounds like somebody's stepping on his bare toes.

I decide to have a look at the crime scene. Before my car pulls out into traffic, I flip through the scribbling in my notebook and discover that the gang rumble took place on Pacific Avenue. Hmm, Pacific—hardly a peaceful place for a rumble. Arriving on the scene, I find our illustrious deputy assistant fire marshal hooking a fire hose up to the local doggie-land's message central. The marshal is still tightening the hydrant coupling, when I appeal to his better nature to let me examine the crime scene before he washes everything to smithereens and puddles.

"Listen, bub," the pot-bellied crew-cut says. "I got orders from headquarters to clean up the street here. See?"

"Sure, but five or ten minutes later won't matter."

"I got a schedule to keep—there's a gasoline spill on Church Street and an accident over on Planter Street and Ward."

I offer up my last Snickers bar, and the guy scans the horizon before snatching it out of my hands. He peels back the wrapper, chomps down, and through chocolate-smeared teeth mumbles, "Okay. You got ten minutes, no more."

Two separate bloody places mark the murder scene. The larger one is pooled, most likely from the victim's knife wound. The other is a jagged streak on the curb. I figure it's where Peter hit his head. Or where the victim's blood splattered from the attacker's blow. A long splinter lies wedged in the grooves of a nearby manhole cover. It looks like it came from the side of a baseball bat. I pry it loose with my penknife and stick it in a brown paper lunch bag from the car. There're also a few muddy footprints on the macadam street.

Just as I attempt to remove a smelly sneaker hiding inside the storm drain, I hear, "Time's up!" I look over at the deputy assistant marshal who has a mile-wide grin. He's turning on the water. The stream hits me in the gut, flips me onto my butt, and sweeps me into the gutter. The obnoxious grin has grown into a full guffaw. I can see his beer belly jiggling up and down to some unknown polka beat. I'm a mess—not only soaking wet, but full of mud and assorted gutter gunk. I swear I'll get even with this fire department funnyman when I submit a cleaning bill to his boss. Even if they don't pay, he'll get a dishonorable mention with the city officials, and maybe they'll dock his pay. I only wish.

I pick myself up and squeegee off as best as I can. Spreading the morning fish-wrapper on my Buick's seat, I drive back to the office for a fresh set of clothes. I enter my illustrious establishment expecting to hear a friendly "Aw, poor guy" from my secretary. Instead, I find Vo giggling behind one hand and my ex-brother-in-law sitting on my Castro Convertible couch, hee-hawing away.

I give the stink eye to Vo. She drops the smirking routine and picks up on her typing. It's got to be her homework; I haven't given her any dictation for days.

"What the hell are you doing here?" I crab at Elmer.

"Have I got a deal for you," he blurts out, while trying to morph into a believable dealmaker.

"What is it this time? No, don't tell me. It'll wait until I change into dry clothes." I slip into what Vo politely calls the office powder room. Ten minutes later I emerge in gym shorts and T-shirt. Elmer starts laughing again, and this time he gets the stink-eye from me.

I plop the sopping clothes on the floor next to Vo's desk, to which the broad responds, "I don't do windows or laundry, Slim, you know that! We agreed."

"This time you owe me," I reply. "You ridiculed me, Vo, when I came in the door. Besides, I can't go out on the street dressed like this. All I'm asking is that you take my things to Soo Fat's Laundry around the corner."

"But you look so cute in knobby knees and hairy legs. You should wear shorts all the time."

"I'm warning you, Vo."

"Okay, Okay." Vo doesn't repent, but stuffs the lot into a plastic bag and heads out the door, chuckling all the way.

I turn to Elmer. "What do you want from me this time, you parasitic weasel?"

"My, aren't we grumpy today."

"I've got a right to be grumpy, the way my day is going."

"Tell me about it," he says. "Maybe I can help."

"So now you're an amateur psychoanalyst? Do you rent your couch by the day or week, you conniving chiseler?"

"Whoa thar, Trigger. I take it you're still sore over the deal I got you on the new bed."

"Some deal that was. The frame only had three casters. The box spring had sprung coils, and the mattress felt like genuine horse feathers."

"I threw in a book just the right size for the missing caster, didn't I?"

"You're full of compassion and generosity, Elmer. No, I'm not still mad at you for that."

"Then what's wrong, Slim."

I tell Elmer all about how Fawn turned me down in my

hour of need.

He seems to listen sympathetically. "Hey, Slim," he finally says. "I've got my own connection in the prosecutor's office."

"You having an in with one of the ADAs is about as likely as flying pork chops," I reply.

"No. Someone even better than that."

"Who, then?"

"Mimi Hedenbacher," he announces. "Just who you need."

"And she's a lawyer, a clerk, or a secretary?"

"None of those. But Mimi can unlock any door or cabinet you want in that office."

"Just what does she do for that office?"

"She's the building custodian, a janitor."

"And just how is a damn custodian gonna help me?"

"She's got the keys to all the doors."

"What about the file cabinets?" I ask. "We gotta get into them to see Peter's file."

"Well, Mimi did some time for breaking and entry. She's real good at picking cabinet locks, too. Been doing it for the two years since she got out of the slammer."

"Whoa!" I say. "How does an ex-con get a job with keys to the prosecutor's office?"

"By periodically doin' some light snitch work for one of the ADAs. Don't worry, Mimi won't snitch on you—she's got scruples."

Elmer's got an answer for everything. "How do you know she'll do this for me?"

"For fifty small ones, she'll unlock anything. Leave it to me. I'll arrange everything. Tonight at ten, okay?"

"Yeah, but don't tell Vo. She won't go for anything illegal, and I won't get the fifty from her to pay Mimi."

* * *

I get to the George P. Frenklyn Municipal Annex Building on Main Street a few minutes to ten that night. Mimi is nowhere in sight, so I climb the steps to the big glass doors. The hall beyond is dimly lit. Suddenly, there's a pair of eyes, big and bloodshot, staring out at me through the glass. I hear the lock jiggle, and the door swings inward.

Mimi is not what I expect. She's a handsome woman in her late forties, but enormously overweight; curly shredded-wheat hair, and dressed in denim coveralls with boondocker shoes. She smiles at me through a missing tooth. "Slim?"

"Mimi?"

"Yeah!"

She locks the front door behind me, and the next thing I know I'm being led to the elevator. On the third floor we step out into a hall, turn right, and we're in prosecutor country. One glass-paneled door later, there's a mop and pail sitting on a little wheeled platform outside the office of Howard E. Browning. She unlocks the door, flicks on the light, and rolls her cleaning gear inside. I head for the wall of filing cabinets and spy the one drawer marked S-SL. With a pair of probes she tinkers with the cabinet lock, and in two shakes, the drawer slides open. I run my Latex glove over the folders, and sure enough, there's a tab labeled "Scalapini, Peter." But there's no file in the hanging folder. At that moment we hear someone in the hall. I can see the shadow approaching through the opaque glass wall to the hall.

Mimi follows it too and calmly begins to sing "Lambs to the Altar" in her soulful soprano voice, all the while shoving me behind her. Mimi accomplishes two things using her enormous tuchus, One, she shoves me against the cabinet, forcing the drawer shut. Two, she provides a cover no one could possibly see beyond. I hear the door open. Mimi is still singing while swishing the mop back and forth over the vinyl tiles, using only her arms. Her hips, bulging like risen yeast dough, cover me, pressing me against the cabinet. Meanwhile, I get the tsunami shakes. What if the person comes in and takes a closer look? I could get five years in the can for this.

"Oh, it's you, Mimi," a friendly man's voice says. "Keep up the good work. Goodnight." The intruder leaves, and his shadow moves down the hall. A minute later, we hear the elevator doors open and close.

"Whew!" I utter. "That was a close one." Then, I do an immediate handlectomy and remove the drawer from my stinging arse. I open the drawer and find the hanging folder again. "The file ain't in there," I say aloud.

"Try the big drawer on Browning's desk," Mimi offers. "It's been my expert custodial experience that some people keep their more current goodies in their desk file drawer. She's already there picking the desk lock for me. In thirty seconds the drawer's open and, sure enough, the file's there just like Mimi predicted. I lay the folder down on the steel desk, turn on the green study lamp, and peruse the first few pages of "boilerplate," while Mimi skates through the office with her damp mop in a lick-and-a-promise mode. Then I come across the coroner's report and a bunch of crime scene photographs.

The report describes a wound made from the downward thrust of a knife; it fits the description of the knife discovered at the crime scene. The report uses a lot of medical mumbo-jumbo, but the gist is that the cause of death for one Manuel, aka Manny-the-Snake, Lopez is a short-term, massive bleed-out. It's just what I expected, so I keep on reading. There's a whole raft of photos stuffed in the back of the file. One, of Peter lying unconscious, catches my attention, but for the life of me, I can't figure out why.

Another photo is a blowup of the supposed murder weapon. I examine it very closely and discover that the bone-handled blade has the initials P and G faintly scratched into it. I'm betting ADA Browning is assuming the P and G stand for Peter and some middle initial or nickname.

A half-hour later, I figure that I've seen and read enough, so I return the file folder to the desk file drawer. I turn to Mimi, who is now emptying trash baskets. A swift but gentle potch-un-tuchas gets her attention. I pay her, and she stuffs the fifty smackers I'd weaseled out of Vo into her super-size bra, and plants a whopper of a sloppy kiss on my cheek. Armed with the few facts that I gleaned, I retreat from the Municipal Annex building in a hurry.

First thing the next morning, I pop into the jail where they're holding Peter and give him the mixed news of my night's adventure. He punches the air with his fist and a resounding "Yes! How soon do I get out?"

"Slow down, kid. Even if we've got something, it may take time for your lawyer to legally discover all this evidence."

"But, Mr. Wittz, you know I didn't do it. Can't we show them the evidence we have?"

"No way. The court can't know the tricks I used to peek at this evidence or I'll get into a whole heap of trouble myself. I could go to the slammer for it. Your lawyer will have to wade through all the legal-beagle stuff. You gotta be patient. You can't get around the legal discovery process."

"That's unfair," he pouts, his shoulders slumping.

"I suppose it is from your point of view. By the way, do you know anyone else in the Barons whose first name begins with P?"

"Yeah. There's Pasquale Gramaldi and… uh… Pauli Raphello. Why?"

"The knife most likely belongs to your friend Pasquale. Does he have it in for you, kid?"

"He's no friend of mine! We went a few rounds last week over some name he called me. Pasquale gave me this scab over my right eye and I gave him a bloody nose, so he was still plenty pissed when a couple a Falcons came and broke up our fight. He ran off screaming he'd get even. Say, how do you know the knife belongs to him?"

"The initials P and G are scratched into the blade," I tell him.

"Yellow bone handle about so long?" He gestures, hands about eight inches apart.

I nod.

"It's his all right," says Peter.

"By the way," I ask, "what's your relationship with Manny Lopez?"

"The kook doesn't have all his marbles. The nut case accused me of ratting him out to his parole officer that he was on drugs. I told him I wasn't the squealer. We pushed and shoved for a few minutes, and then I knocked him off his feet. That was pretty much it."

"Were there any witnesses to that scuffle?"

"Yeah," Peter mumbled. "At least half the Falcons were there. Can they use that against me?"

"I'm afraid so."

I leave the kid in slightly lower spirits than when I found him. In the car once more, I use the cell phone to set up a meeting with Gepetto and Wilber Ginzberg, the court-appointed lawyer.

Three hours later, I'm sitting in the barber chair facing the two of them, who are seated in the rattan waiting chairs. Wilber's neat clipped curly black hair, stern hazel eyes, and sharply pressed pinstripe suit just might prove an asset in Peter's case. I present everything I've learned to the two men and answer a number of questions.

Wilber says he'll file for immediate discovery of all charges and evidence the prosecutor possesses and, if all is in order, he will request a pretrial hearing with the judge. If that happens, he may be able to get the case thrown out before it goes to trial.

"I hope you will protect the source of this information, Mr. Ginzberg," I impress upon him.

"For a $200 retainer I can take you on as a client, and all that you have told me becomes privileged attorney-client information."

He sees the dumb where-did-that-come-from expression on my face and starts to laugh. "Not to worry, Mr. Wittz. I'm joking. There's no reason to believe your name would ever come up in a pretrial hearing. I'm entitled to full disclosure, which includes everything you've seen in those files. The discovery then becomes the source. Your somewhat dubious methods should achieve the desired result. Thank you."

I like this young lawyer's approach. His aggressiveness can't hurt either.

* * *

It takes nearly three weeks for the prosecutor to get off his butt and schedule a pretrial hearing. It's an open hearing, so I plop myself down in the first-row gallery close to the defense table. A couple of rows behind me I recognize some of the Falcons from my 'hood. I know some of them have been subpoenaed by the defense. From the looks of the collection of budding thugs on the opposite side of the gallery, I'm guessing they're Barons. I see one that fits the description of Pasquale Gramaldi, complete with an old knife scar on his left cheek. There's even one bozo in the bunch that could play linebacker for the Rams all by hisself. I lean over the rail to ask, and Peter nods a Yes, it's Bully Mahone.

The hearing begins with the coroner reading from her report, and she demonstrates the penetration thrust—downward. Then ADA Browning presents his crime scene evidence to the judge, stressing two photos: one with the knife in Peter's hand, and the other, a close-up of the knife focusing on the initials. He emphasizes the P for Peter several times. Also, one Falcon and two Baron witnesses testify to a physical confrontation between the defendant and the deceased. Browning points out Peter's recent wounds. The ADA is cleverly building a case for an internal beef—one not involving the Barons at all. Overall, it looks pretty grim for our side. Peter is scowling, and his arms are crossed over his chest, hands balled into fists. He's trying to keep his cool.

While Browning punctuates his case, Wilbur is studying a photo that he has propped up in front of him: the damning photo of Peter holding the knife. I can see it as well. Suddenly, it hits me up the side of the head—why this photo is so significant. I lean over the rail and whisper in Wilber's ear. He nods and releases the hint of a small smile.

Now it's his turn to rebut. He takes a letter opener from his briefcase and asks the ADA to grip the opener in either hand in the manner of the first photo, that is, with the blade facing the same direction as the thumb. "Now, sir, try a downward thrusting motion." Browning tries with first the right hand and then the left, but he can't seem to turn the blade over more than forty-five degrees to stab downward.

"Then wouldn't you say the knife is a plant?" asks Ginzberg.

"Maybe!" replies the frustrated ADA. "But that still doesn't mean he didn't stab the Lopez kid. In the photo it looks like Scalapini is holding the knife in a defensive position ready to take on his next victim."

Wilbur fires back. "His fingers are closely wrapped around the knife. Wouldn't you think he'd relax his fingers some after being knocked cold with a baseball bat from behind?"

"Again, maybe." the ADA grudgingly admits.

Next, Wilbur calls Pasquale Gramaldi to the witness stand and asks, first, for his full name and, second, for his initials. The stocky, pimply faced Pasquale complies. Then Wilbur asks Pasquale if he knows who the defendant is and gets a vigorous nod.

"Yeah," Pasquale says. "We butted heads a couple a times, had some classes together, too."

"Do you know his full name?"

Pasquale replies, "Pietro Scalapini, but they call him Petey."

"And his initials?" the lawyer pushes.

"P.S. just like in letters," Pasquale replies with a smirk.

"P.S.," Ginzberg repeats. "Then this knife is more likely to be yours than Peter's. Isn't that so?" He shoves the evidence bag containing the knife right under Pasquale's nose.

"Yeah. It's mine, all right, but I didn't cut nobody, and besides, I ain't seen that shiv since last Wednesday night."

"Then you're claiming someone stole it?" asked Wilbur.

"Naw!" Pasquale mumbled. "I lent it out."

I can hardly hear Pasquale on account of the rising din generated in the right rear gallery. Out of the ruckus a bellowing voice bursts out: "Keep your mouth shut if you know what's good for you."

The judge slams the gavel down hard like it's a sledgehammer. "One more outburst and I'll clear the courtroom."

I doubt that the judge heard the threat or he would have emptied the joint already. Wilber continues unshaken.

"Who did you lend the knife to?"

An uneasy shuffle ferments in the right rear gallery, but subsides as soon as the judge picks up his gavel and glares at them.

"I don't known," Pasquale whispers.

"You don't know or you won't tell the court?"

"I can't tell."

"And why is that?"

"I'm a dead man if I tell."

"You'd rather do time for murder or conspiracy to commit murder than tell who you lent the knife to?"

Beads of sweat pop out on Pasquale's upper lip. His Adam's apple does a dance in his neck. "I didn't cut nobody. I don't want to do time. He did the cutting. He killed Manny-the-Snake. At first, I didn't know why he wanted my knife. He practically took it from me so's he could do the cutting. He said his sister was dating a Falcon—it was his honor at stake. Pretty bone-headed reason to off someone, if you ask me. I had nuttin' to do with this killing."

"You rat-fink-bastard. I'll get you for this!" A Godzilla of a figure leaps up from the gallery and charges for the door.

"It's Bully Mahone!" Peter cries out.

"Y'er a dead man, Gramaldi," booms the retreating mountain over his shoulder.

"It's Bully Mahone" repeats Pasquale, "and I'm a dead man."

"Stop him!" yells the judge. Two uniforms appear at the door and attempt to apprehend Bully. They only manage to slow down his bull rush. It takes a third uniform to restrain and cuff him. They take him away.

ADA Browning finally announces that he no longer has a

viable case against Peter Scalapini. Upon hearing this, the judge dismisses the case and orders Peter's immediate release.

At sentencing, twenty-eight-year-old Bully Mahone becomes a guest of the state for the next twenty-five years. In a separate plea agreement, Pasquale gets a five-year sentence for conspiracy; the suspension is for his cooperation in convicting Bully. He is also given a free train ticket to anywhere in the country that he chooses. Peter learns from Pasquale's parole officer that Pasquale is the one who ratted Manny out on the drug charge. A pretty gutsy guy, if you ask me.

* * *

The Scalapini family, Wilber, and myself celebrate the victory in the Scalapini apartment upstairs from the barbershop. Vo is invited and shows up, too. Wilber accepts a lifetime of free haircuts as his fee and, reluctantly, so do I. Peter announces that he got a job at a local hardware store, and has renounced his membership in the Falcons. Everyone cheers but Vo.

"What's wrong?" I ask her.

"Since you accepted haircuts for a fee, how am I going to get a paycheck out of that?"

"Vo, how much do you spend on your hair every month?" I ask.

"Between fifty and sixty dollars. Why?"

Gepetto, now back to his jolly self, interrupts. "I do that for free. I color. I style. I cut and I trim. I do good job. Ask anybody."

Vo's scarlet lips shift from a pout to a smile. "Well, okay then. I guess I'm stuck with Slim and trim." She waves goodbye with her lacquered nails and disappears out the door.

I sidle up to Gepetto. "Hey, friend, this is good news. I didn't know you do all that stuff for the ladies."

Gepetto breaks into a guilty grin. "I don't. But I make a my way."

#

Slim Jim

I'VE BEEN KNOWN TO WAKE UP in some pretty strange places, mind you. Anyplace would be better than the Castro Convertible in my office—well, almost anyplace. Some dame's boudoir would've been nice. A sluggish brain compels me to make sense of the immediate swirling world. One eye slowly focuses and then the other. I discover apartment brick walls on three sides, and the forth—way off in the distance, a narrow opening onto a street. A cab passes quickly, an old man strolls by, and a drunk ducks in, relieves himself, and vanishes once more. The back of my head is screaming, my voice is drowning in cotton, and the rest of me aches. Something else smells.

I roll to one side and manage to sit upright. Then I realize it's the stench of alcohol, and it's coming from me—all over the front of my cardigan. I don't drink any more because my heart doc says that's a no-no. Someone has worked me over pretty good, then poured the juice down my front. My wallet and watch are gone. If this is supposed to be a mugging, the booze doesn't figure. I brush the alley dirt from my slacks and try to stand up, holding on to the nearest brick wall with one hand and a wooden crate with the other. The woozies return and I stumble into a GI can. After a few minutes the ground under me finally comes into balance, where I can stand on my own.

I bend down to pick up my hat. It was a nice Bogie-type fedora this morning; now it's been flattened by a freakin' footprint. Not three feet away, I spot a woman's spiked-heel patent leather pump. What's odd is that it looks new, not what you'd expect in dumpsterville. As I bend down again to get a better look, I see a second shoe—this one with a foot still in it, plus a well-shaped leg. Now I'm getting creeped out.

Dragging myself around the wooden crate, I discover this broad lying curled in a tight fetal position in the shadows facing the wall. With the back of my hand I try to turn her head toward me, but the body is so wedged against the bricks I can't move it. All I can do is kneel and grab her wrist. No pulse.

No wonder. There's a hole in the back of her brunette head the size of Delaware, though there ain't enough blood to fill a shot glass. Which means she was murdered somewhere else and unloaded in the alley. The lady looks to be thirtyish, slender body, and I have a bad feeling it may be a former client of mine. Her black silk suit, plus the nice shoes—the clothes spell money. No jewelry, and her outfit's not torn or roughed up at all. I'm thinking robbery, not rape. I'm about to straighten up when my sore knee hits a thick hard object. I grab hold of it. What the hell? I pull my hand back. It's a gun, a snub-nosed .38-caliber revolver—better known as a mail-order Saturday Night Special.

Now I'm smelling something else and it ain't booze. Getting mugged was no random act. I've been set up.

I'll lay ya five-to-one odds that piece has my prints all over it. As a licensed private eye, my prints are on file. My reputation is at stake here and I'm in a dilemma, big time . If I leave the gun for the police, I become the numero uno chump for this dame's demise. If I wipe the piece clean, I'll be destroying the perp's prints, and the most valuable piece of evidence is lost forever. I figure I gotta be more resourceful, so I dig around in the GI can and come up with just the things I need. I use a derelict ice cream paddle to push the gun onto last Tuesday's sport page and wrap the .38 and the paddle up in one tight package. I cram the bundle into my cardigan pocket and stagger down the long, narrow alley to the street.

The streetlamp's glare hurts my eyes, but at least I recognize where I am. I wish I could remember how I got here, though. It's at least fifteen blocks to my office. I must have driven, but my Buick Regal ain't anywhere to be seen—so maybe not. I dig deep into my pockets and come up with a quarter, two dimes, a buffalo nickel, a cough drop, and three Lincoln pennies—not enough for a bus, let alone a cab. It's well past sunset, which means my secretary has left for her night school law classes. I drag myself one more block and I'm certain there ain't another ten aching steps left in my legs.

I spot a phone booth and my lips part in irony—there's only one person I can call at this hour, my ex-brother-in-law, El-mer. When Fawn and I divorced, she got the furniture and I got Elmer.

Maybe you're wondering why I don't call the police to tell 'em about the body. Because if they find me here, in my present condition they won't believe a word outta my mouth. Can't say I'd blame them; I wouldn't believe me either. And of course there's the gun thing.

Which leaves Elmer. He's always trying to sell me some-thing I don't want or need. When I do get sucked in, I usually wind up with one of his "I can get it for you cheaper" bargains. Like the secure, five-drawer filing cabinet that came with a chubby screwdriver jammed into the lock and the middle drawer stuck in the out position.

I squeeze into the phone booth and look for the phone book. Of course there isn't one. That would be too easy. I need Elmer's number, so I drop my lone quarter in the slot, punch in four-one-one and wait. A choppy feminine computerized voice an-swers, "May I help you? What number do you want?"

"Elmer Petrious on Maple Street, please." I spell out the last name.

"There's no listing for Elmer Petrious on Maple Street, sir, but we do have an Ellen Patriot on Maple Street."

"Try Effie Petrious." I'm thinking it may be listed in Elmer's wife's name.

"There's no listing for an Effie Petrious either, but we do have an Effie Parsons on Elm Street. Are you sure of the street or the spelling, sir?"

"Yeah, I'm certain of both. Try looking again."

"Well, there's an Eddie Petrie on Blare Place, a Matilda Petrie on Second Avenue, and a Mrs. Louis Peonea on Fleet Street."

"Cut that out. You're not helping. I want my quarter back."

"Sir, I don't like your tone. And you can't have it back. You've completed this call."

"Let me talk to your supervisor, ma'am."

"I'm not a ma'am, sir. A computer is what I am, and we don't have supervisors."

"Well, somebody has to be in charge."

"That would be the data base manager, sir."

"Let me talk with him, then." Elevator music suddenly fills the receiver, so loud I have to hold it away from my ear. I wait at least four minutes before a human voice answers.

"Sorry for the delay. How may I help you?" It's a masculine voice, a real one this time.

I explain my problem in detail, and he does a search and comes up with the only Petrious listed. Bingo! It's my ex-mother-in-law. So I ask to be connected, and he tells me I have to make another call. I memorize the number and hang up. I put in the two dimes and a nickel and punch in the number. This leaves me with three pennies and a cough drop. I can hear the ringing in the background and then "Hello."

"Hi, Mom, it's me, Slim. I'm stuck on the other side of town without any cash. I tried to call Elmer, but his number ain't listed."

"Oh, Slim, Elmer's is unlisted. You know how he is. Creditors are always dunning him."

"Mom, can you call him and have him pick me up on the

corner of Twenty-third and Main?"

She cares about me and wants to know all the bloody details.

"Mom, I'd love to chat, but I hurt all over and need to get to bed. Ask Elmer to hurry, please!"

"You poor dear. Of course."

Rush hour is long past and there's hardly any traffic. Every set of headlights gets my hopes up. After what seems like an hour, a small single light approaches. It veers across the road in a U-turn, then stops at the curb. I see it's one of those Cushman motor scooters with Elmer seated atop of it. He's got a grin as wide as a dinner plate.

"Hi, Slim. I got here as soon as soon as I could. My Chevy's in the shop, so I took Effie's wheels. C'mon, climb aboard."

"Where do I sit on this damn thing?"

He shimmies forward on the longish seat, and I mount the seat behind him. After bouncing my sore bones across town, Elmer drops me off at my office. I climb the stairs to the second floor, unlock the door, and shed the cardigan, gun, and shoes in the middle of the floor. Next I head for the dreaded Castro Convertible. It wasn't so bad when I bought it, but now it's feels like a combo of rocks and corrugated cardboard. Never mind. I lie down, kick off my shoes, and stretch. If you ask what's next, I can't tell you—I'm totally out of it.

* * *

Garish sunlight penetrates my eyelids and tortures me awake just in time to hear the office door swing open. Vo plops the morning paper and a purse the size of a small Jeep on top of her desk. She stops in the middle of the floor and attempts to pick up my cardigan, where I dropped it last night, but the piece weighs it down. She removes the package from the sweater pocket and feels through the newspaper wrapping.

"Whoa, there, Slim, are you packing heat now?" she asks as her fingers start to unravel the gun.

"Don't touch it," I yell as I fly off the couch and my feet hit the floor. "It might be evidence." All the aches and pains from the night before return like a barreling freight train.

She shoots me a confused look and lays the partially wrapped package on my desk. "Either it's evidence or it's not. Which is it, Slim?"

"If the prints on the piece are mine, it's a frame-up, not evidence," I tell her. "If the prints belong to someone else, it's evidence. Does that make sense?" When she arches one penciled eyebrow, I can tell it doesn't, so I give her the lowdown on my waking up in the alley behind an apartment house. She begins shaking her head the minute I start, so I say, "What?"

"You can get into big trouble with the law, withholding evidence like this." It's Vo's second-year law school scolding me now. She spreads open the newspaper wrapper on my desk. Then she opens her purse and removes a rhinestone-covered compact. Using the powder puff inside, she dusts the grip, trigger, guard, and barrel. The only prints that show up are one clear thumbprint on the smooth left side of the grip and a bunch of partial digit prints below it. We both agree that it's a right-handed shooter. The bad news is that when Vo presses my thumb down on the desktop glass and dusts the spot, the thumbprints match. The good news is I'm a lefty. Someone—I have no idea who—is setting me up for the murder.

I confess to Vo: "I can't even remember how I got to the alley or why I went to that neighborhood in the first place. Did I take the Buick?"

Vo snaps her compact shut. "You left here saying you were taking the bus—going to warn Bugs Foggle's wife that he was released from prison yesterday. Apparently, Bugs is looking to get even with Betty for her testimony leading to his incarceration. He got early parole after ten years' good behavior."

I stroke my prickly chin, badly in need of a shave. Nice of Vo to ignore it. "Yeah," I said, "I remember knocking on Betty's door, then nothing. I woke up in the alley with this." I gently pat the knot on my head. It's bigger than a Ping Pong ball.

Vo has more important things on her mind than my wound. "Well, Slim, how do you propose to get this gun to the police?"

"Do we have to?" I ask. She gives me an *Are you nuts?* look, and I reluctantly agree. "How about we mail it—anonymously?"

"But it has your fingerprints on it, Slim, and powder traces from my puff. They'll nail you for evidence tampering if not for the murder itself."

"Powder traces! That's it, gal."

"That's what?"

"We wipe the gun clean with an oil rag. Then I bring the gun in myself and volunteer for a gunpowder residue test."

"But that's evidence tampering too, Slim. You just can't do that."

"I didn't kill anybody—let alone Betty Foggle, if it is Betty, so it's not real evidence anyway."

"What makes you think the body is hers?"

"I don't know for sure. I couldn't see her face, and it's been years since I did a little gumshoeing for her. Where's that morning paper you brought in?"

Vo rushes over to her desk and begins flipping through the pages. "Here it is, on page four under Police Beat. They found an unidentified woman's body in an alley off Twenty-second Street."

"So the cops don't know who she is either," I say. "Well, here's the plan. I'm going drop off the clean gun, in a way that both the powder puff and I will remain anonymous. That will give me some time to investigate on my own."

In her clingy purple mini-dress Vo looks like she's ready for a date, but the words out of her mouth are stern. "Don't tell me! I don't want to know. I'm out of the loop, Slim. Remember, I know nothing at all."

"Yeah, sure. You're innocent as a newborn babe."

I put on fresh Latex gloves, and in the next half hour, I oil the piece and wipe it clean. When it glistens, I put it in a double lunch-size brown bag and walk the three blocks to the nearest police precinct. Inside, it's teeming with noise and activity, so I easily amble past the desk sergeant like I belong there and wander the halls looking for the first empty room. Luckily, no one sees me park the bag on someone's bookcase. I make a clean getaway and head down the street to pick up my beat-up Buick Regal.

As I near the lot, I see Fish-Face Eddie hanging over my car, arguing with someone inside it. Getting closer, I make out the face of a teenage female with disheveled blonde hair and a freckled face that looks like it hasn't been washed in a week. Eddie's yelling some words at the girl that would make an ex-con blush. She's sitting in the driver's seat, staring straight ahead, with her fists clenched in the pockets of a bulky navy-blue sweatshirt. Nothing unusual about that except that it's July and already about eighty degrees out.

"Hey, Eddie! Who's the girl and what's she doing in my car? I don't want to hear that you're renting it out to teenagers now."

"I don't know who or why," he yelps at me. "All I know is she got inside and locked all the doors. Hold on, Slim, I'll get her out for you."

He picks up a tire iron and starts to swing at the window. "Whoa there, Eddie!" I grab his arm and yank it away. "Ain't there some other way to get the door open without smashing in the window?"

Fish-Face grumbles and heads back to his four-by-four shed at the front of the lot. Meanwhile, I try my own brand of reason and persuasion on the teenage intruder. Being nice to her doesn't help. She still stares rigidly out the windshield, but I notice twitching muscles in her neck, and a clenched belligerent jaw. No makeup, but fullish lips severely pinched together. She's more angry than scared.

Eddie reappears, this time with a Slim-Jim, an illegal tool for breaking into cars. He slips the flat sheet-metal device between the glass and the felt window liner on the door and tries to fit one of the notches in the device to the internal door lock mechanism. A few minutes pass while he finds the right notch and the right place to use it. Finally, I see the door lock button rising inside the window. Success, I think.

Nope. It takes two hands to pull the Slim-Jim and the button up. As soon as he lets go to open the door handle, whoa! The girl's left hand flies up and slams the button down again. Good reflexes, The game of up/down goes on for a bunch until I step in and work the door handle while Eddie pulls up on the tool.

With the door swung wide, I repeat the word "Out" several times in successively more gruff, commanding tones, but the brat ignores me. I try pulling her out by her arm, but she's strong and uses her athleticism to twist away. I quickly squeeze one arm behind her back and the other under her legs and start to heft her out of the car. Her deadpan face refreezes in rage and her unfolding muscular arms batter about my head. When that doesn't work, her long nails dig into my cheek. The sharp pain makes me lose control, and I drop her about a foot onto the tarmac.

Rage begins to melt into a pitiful expression of defeat, followed by a gallon of genuine tears. I unleash the prescribed amount of patience and then offer her my hand to help her up.

"Don't you touch me, you murderer you!"

Now that's a shocker, if I ever heard one. "Why in hell would you say that?" I ask.

"I saw you kill that lady over on Twenty-second Street. You shot her in the head. I saw you do it"

"I didn't shoot her and I can prove it. "The prints on the gun were from a right-hander and I'm a lefty. Besides," I now lie to her, "I passed the gunshot residue test, so I couldn't have fired the gun." Her face goes blank, and she's at a loss for words, so out come the tears again. I sit down on the tarmac and put my arm around her shoulders. This time she doesn't resist.

Meanwhile, Fish-Face Eddie pulls a high-fashion Coach purse from the front seat and starts to go through it, coming up with a wallet and identification. "Looks like this kid's name is Betty Foggle. Right?" He shoves the wallet in her face.

"Wrong!" She sits up and snaps back.

"Eddie, how old is this Ms. Foggle?" I ask.

"Her driver's permit says she's thirty-three."

I help the red-eyed teenager to her feet.

"You need to answer a few questions, young lady. With straight answers. What's your name? How old are you. How do you know so much about that dead woman? And how did you get hold of Betty Foggle's purse?" The teenager begins to tremble and the words blubber out. I wrap her in my arms and she leans on my shoulder. Realizing I could be sending her the wrong message, I straighten her up, look her in the eye and say "I'm waiting."

"My name is Danielle Foggle," she murmers, "and I'll be seventeen next month. Betty is my stepmom." Her voice notches up about two shrill octaves. "It was her lying testimony that sent my father away for a ten- to fifteen-year sentence. That bitch took part in the armed robbery and she was the one who shot the cashier. It was all her idea in the first place. My father didn't want to have any part in the robbery, but she threatened to leave him if he didn't go along."

"And Bugs took the fall for her?"

Danielle's eyes flash. "Yes! Now that bitch Betty is running around with some other guy from that club where she works."

She starts to sob again. I reach out and snatch the purse from Eddie, whose itchy fingers are already counting the bills inside. I'm thinking maybe I should take Danielle back to the office where Vo could add the much needed motherly touch. I walk my charge the three blocks with her leaning on me like I'm her only lifeline.

Vo takes over like the simpatico person she is. A trip to the ladies room and a washed face later, Danielle is seated across my desk from me.

But none of this is making sense. She called me a murderer. Enough Mr. Nice Guy. Is this little girl on the level or the next Sarah Bernhardt? I unleash my questions. "You set me up? You mugged me, took my wallet and watch and Betty's purse?"

Danielle turns her head away slightly with a sheepish look.

"Nice manners you've got, girlie. Aren't you a little young to audition for Ma Barker? Why did you try to pin the murder on me? You didn't even know me."

"You came to my apartment," Danielle snaps. "You knocked on my door. Why? What business was it of yours?"

"When I came to your apartment house, all I wanted to do was warn your stepmother that your father had been released from prison."

I had no idea my client armchair could generate so much thrashing about and stomping. I try to explain without flying off the handle myself. "You were too young to attend the trial, Danielle. I was in the shop when the robbery went down and I testified against your father. I was also there when Bugs swore he'd get even with your stepmom. Yesterday, the arresting officer gave me the heads up about his parole."

"It was too late!" Danielle shrieks. "Betty was already dead. Besides, she didn't deserve to be warned."

I need to ask why, but first things first. The swollen knot on my head is throbbing. "What did you hit me with?"

"The same gun you already have."

"The same gun Bugs shot your stepmom with?"

Danielle shakes her head furiously. "No, no, no! I haven't seen my father since I visited him two weeks ago."

"So what did happen, anyway?" I wait while she gulps from the glass of water Vo brought her.

"Coming home yesterday, I caught Betty going through my father's things, looking for the cash from the robbery. That snake didn't know my father surrendered the loot at his arraignment. When she boasted that she wanted it to run away with her new boyfriend, I smacked her across the face with my hand. Hard, too. Then she tried pulling the gun out of her purse. I grabbed it and we struggled. I pulled her hair, she scratched me on my arm, and both of us went down on the kitchen floor. The gun went off. Blood gushed out of her head all over the place. It was horrible. She wasn't moving—I think she died instantly. I didn't mean to kill her.

All I wanted was to protect myself."

"Are you sure you're not taking the fall for your dad?"

"My dad didn't shoot her. He wasn't there I tell you."

"How did I come into the picture?"

"Once I got over the initial shock," Danielle murmurs, "I devised a plan. I dragged her body out through the rear kitchen door into the alley. It helps that we live in a first-floor apartment. I started to clean up the mess when I heard the doorbell. I stuck the gun in my jeans belt. I had no idea who it was. At first I panicked. I couldn't very well let anyone in. I ran out through the alley, around the building and in through the front entryway—and saw you at our door. I snuck up behind you, pulled the gun out of my jeans, and clobbered you with the handle.

"Then you added me to the garbage collection in the alley?"

"Uh-huh. I figured if you came to visit Betty you had to be a sleazebag."

"Then you went back into your apartment and watched me from the window. When I walked away with the gun, you followed me."

"Yeah, but from way back and I kept ducking into doorways so you wouldn't see me. I saw you go into an office building. I had Betty's purse with me and I knew I had to get rid of it, but I didn't know how. Then I saw this parking lot and all the cars looked pretty decent except a Buick in the back that was real beat up, like who would even want such a junker? But I got spooked—there was a guy in the booth. So I ran home. This morning I walked back to the lot with the purse. I didn't see anybody around. I tried the door to the Buick. It was open! I couldn't believe my luck, so I snuck inside and dropped the purse on the floor. I figured whoever owned the car would get nailed for Betty's murder. I was about to get out and leave, but the lot owner came charging at me and yelling. So I locked the doors."

This is pretty damned creepy, I'm thinking. What were the odds that she'd involve my car? "You're a piece of work, young lady."

"Jeez, if I'd known you were such a nice man I wouldn't have mugged you in the first place. And I sure wouldn't have tried to hang this miserable business on you. How come you have such a crappy car, anyway?"

"That's beside the point. You don't need a private eye. You're starting yourself off with a nice juvy record. What you need is a spanking and a helluva good lawyer. What if I called your father's lawyer?"

"I think he'd want that."

Through the lawyer and parole officer we connect with Bugs Foggle. It takes a few months, but a self-defense plea lands Danielle Foggle a suspended sentence for accidental death. I testify on her behalf, leaving out certain incriminating facts. However, tampering with evidence gets her 600 hours of community service. Apparently, no one figured out how the gun arrived at the police station. It's my little secret.

Back at the office, Vo parks her tush on one corner of my desk, crosses her arms, and looks down at me like a disciplining first grade teacher.

"Slim, you sure screwed up. Why were you schlepping all the way over to Betty's place to warn her? You could have avoided the whole mess with just one handy little gadget that's sitting here on your desk. It was invented by Alexander Graham Bell. Maybe you've heard of him? It's called a telephone."

I hate it when Vo's right.

The End

Also by Rosemary & Larry

The Paco and Molly
Mystery Series

Locks and Cream Cheese—In scandal-ridden Black Rain Corners, a Chesapeake Bay mansion harbors locked rooms and deadly secrets. A wily detective and a gourmet cook tackle the case.

Hot Grudge Sunday—Bank robbers and conspirators derail the sleuths' blissful honeymoon at the Grand Canyon. Can they nail the suspects after they themselves become targets?

Boston Scream Pie—A teenage girl's nightmare triggers a sinister tale of twins, two warring families, and a blonde bombshell who hates being called "Mom."

Available on Amazon.com, Kindle, and Nook.

Also by Rosemary & Larry

Cry Ohana, Adventure and Suspense in Hawaii—A car accident, blackmail, and murder tear apart a Hawaiian ohana (family). Danger erupts at a Filipino wedding, a Maui resort, and the Big Island's volcanic steam vents. Can the family re-unite and bring down the killer?

The Dan and Rivka Sherman Mystery Series (#1)

Death Goes Postal—Rare 15th-century typesetting artifacts journey through time, leaving a horrifying imprint in their wake. Dan and Rivka risk life and limb to locate the treasures and unmask the murderer. Not quite what they expected when they bought The Olde Victorian Bookstore.

The Dan and Rivka Sherman Mystery Series (#2)

Death Takes A Mistress—Daughter of the mistress and her murderous lover, seeking revenge, journeys from London, England to Annapolis, MD to find the killer and her father. But to which family does he belong? Dan and Rivka, owners of The Olde Victorian Bookstore, join in exposing the true villain.

Available on Amazon.com, Kindle, and Nook.

Also by Rosemary

Miriam's World and Mine—Miriam Luby Wolfe, a junior at Syracuse U., spent her fall semester in London exploring her talents: singing, dancing, acting, and writing. But she never made it home. A terrorist bomb destroyed her plane over Lockerbie, Scotland. Learn about Miriam, the Pan Am families, the bombers, and the political fallout.

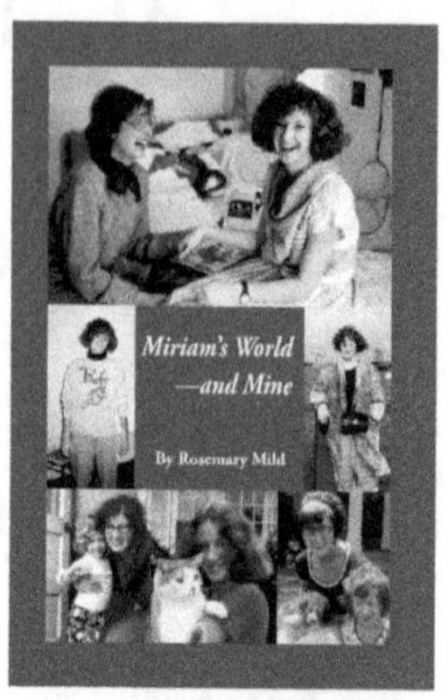

Love! Laugh! Panic! Life with My Mother—Don't we all have mixed emotions about our mothers? Rosemary Mild's mom was super-achieving, but tough to live with. Luby Pollack was a journalist, popular book author, and psychiatrist's wife. Always the Heroine, and sometimes the Villain, from the viewpoint of her loving but ornery daughter.

Available on Amazon.com, Kindle, and Nook.

Photograph by Craig Herndon

Rosemary and Larry Mild coauthor mystery and thriller novels and short stories. Their latest wickedly entertaining short stories appear in new anthologies: ***Mystery in Paradise: 13 Tales of Suspense*** and ***Chesapeake Crimes: Homicidal Holidays***. The Milds recently waved goodbye to Severna Park, Maryland, and moved to Honolulu, Hawaii, where they cherish time with their children and grandchildren.

E-mail the Milds at: roselarry@magicile.com

Visit them at: www.magicile.com